BANDIT LOVE

Massimo Carlotto

BANDIT LOVE

*Translated from the Italian
by Antony Shugaar*

Europa
editions

Europa Editions
116 East 16th Street
New York, N.Y. 10003
www.europaeditions.com
info@europaeditions.com

Copyright © 2009 by Edizioni E/O
First Publication 2010 by Europa Editions

Translation by Antony Shugaar
Original Title: *L'amore del bandito*
Translation copyright © 2010 by Europa Editions

Library of Congress Cataloging in Publication Data is available
ISBN 978-1-933372-80-8

Carlotto, Massimo
Bandit Love

Book design by Emanuele Ragnisco
www.mekkanografici.com

Cover photo © Corbis

Prepress by Plan.ed
www.plan-ed.it

Printed in Canada

BANDIT LOVE

T o the Minister of the Interior, to the Minister of Justice . . .

On March 17th of this year, at the Institute of Legal Medicine of the University of Padua, there was a burglary resulting in the theft of a substantial quantity of illegal narcotics [. . .] the narcotics were being held in the laboratories for toxicological testing of the active principles. The narcotics in question comprised a total weight of approximately forty-four (44) kilograms, subdivided into thirty (30) kilograms of heroin, ten (10) kilograms of cocaine, and the rest in smaller lots of amphetamines, pills and other substances [. . .].

These illegal substances were located in the storerooms of the laboratory of the Institute; access to those storerooms was blocked by an armored door; only those in possession of a magnetic card and accompanying alphanumeric code could enter without triggering the electronic security alarm.

According to media reports, the theft was carried out without any evidence of damage to the locks of the armored doors and by deactivation of the alarm system . . .

Written response to parliamentary inquiry 4-10236
—session no. 476,
Monday, June 14, 2004

The foreigner walked past the plate-glass window of the expensive beauty parlor for the third time. The woman had her back to the mirror. She was selecting a nail polish, nodding distractedly as the manicurist made her recommendations and a hairdresser, aged about fifty, combed her hair with confident precision.

The foreigner walked on, figuring that it wouldn't be much longer before the woman left the shop. He'd been following her for exactly one week now and he sensed that the time was right. He straightened the lapel of his long dark overcoat and stopped in front of another shop window to look at a few antiques, especially a late eighteenth-century table of Venetian manufacture.

The proprietor of the shop was adjusting a painting of an elderly noblewoman. He smiled at the foreigner, encouraging him to enter the shop. The foreigner lowered his head, in an apparently natural way, not as if he were trying to escape notice, and pretended to be deeply interested in a lamp standing on a side table. Then he turned and moved away.

He wasn't worried in the slightest. There hadn't been time for his features to impress themselves in the antiques dealer's mind, and experience had taught him that eyewitnesses are seldom reliable. But above all, his tranquility stemmed from the fact that he was a perfect stranger in a neighborhood that in no more than an hour he would leave, never to return.

He walked on down the porticoed walkway, shooting glances into the fashionable shopfronts, trying to guess where else the woman might make a stop before deciding to return home. She lived in a nearby town, and the foreigner understood perfectly why she had to drive from her town to this one just to have her hair done. The town where she lived was on the water. There was no one there but fishermen and their families; in late October the tourists stopped coming, most of the shops and restaurants closed for the winter, and those few shops that kept their shutters raised were certainly unworthy of the discerning tastes of such an elegant woman.

It was a workday, midafternoon, winter shadows, only the occasional pedestrian . . . The foreigner evaluated the operating conditions once again; as he did, he knocked softly on the side of a white panel van. Before getting in, he stopped to take a quick glance at the small expensive car parked right next to it.

"I don't think we'll have much longer to wait," he told the two men seated on the boxes that cluttered the van's cargo deck.

Neither man moved a muscle or made the slightest sound. They were professionals; they had no use for theories or possibilities. They'd been ready for a while now, and they'd be ready until the job was done. The foreigner knew them well; they were his most trusted accomplices. Years ago, in the army, they'd had ranks and uniforms, but now they were just a pair of faithful heavies, his enforcers and, when needed, capable killers.

The glare of a nearby streetlight filtered through the heavy paper covering the windows of the rear cargo doors. The foreigner glanced at the hands of his two lieutenants; they were gloved in latex: in that dim light they had taken on a spectral hue. The gloves on his own hands were made of a fine, thin leather. None of the three men wanted to leave fingerprints behind; and they wouldn't. The panel van would drive for a long way until it reached safe haven, but they would set fire to it anyway, to keep even the finest scrap of fiber or drop of biological evidence from falling into the hands of a prying detective.

The foreigner knew that he was being far too careful, but he had too little information about the motives and interests that had summoned him to that town in Northeast Italy to let down his guard. He had been contacted and paid a very substantial sum of money to take care of that woman. A contract like any other. Simple and straightforward: but he had survived a civil war, and as far as he was concerned he was still alive because he'd always been careful about details.

He heaved a sigh and got comfortable.

The woman continued to chat with the manicurist as she walked to the cash register. The hairdresser took just one more lingering look at her ass. Not only was it a nice ass, the woman knew how to make it undulate and sway. The hairdresser's appraising stare did not escape his wife, who was blow-drying another customer's hair. Without missing a beat, she savored the vicious comment she planned to hiss at him the minute the woman was out the door. "That black bitch is nothing but a whore," would be the first words out of her mouth. They were vicious words; they were also substantially inaccurate. The woman's skin was amber and her eyes were blue, the sort of combination you'd expect to find when an Arab woman from Sétif, Algeria, decides to have a baby with a Breton from St.-Malo, France. She was just under 5' 8", but her high-heeled boots made her look taller; her body was firm and supple, and her movements were sensual and lithe, the movements of the belly dancer that she was. She had been performing professionally for over a quarter century, in nightclubs all over Europe: that was why the hairdresser's wife was eagerly waiting to call her a slut. The fact is that most of the men around there liked the woman's looks, even the younger men, who would have gladly slipped into bed with that exotic forty-six-year-old dancer from another country.

As she waited for the credit card receipt to print out, the woman took a look at herself in the mirror, turning her head ever so slightly so that her long raven hair bounced, shimmering with auburn highlights. She crossed the street and stepped into a coffee shop. She ordered her usual blend and savored the little cup of espresso, leaving a perfect lipstick kiss on the rim of the demitasse. She conversed briefly with the proprietor, an habitué of the nightclub where she worked. He showed her a brochure advertising a bellydancing class, and suggested she ask about teaching. She said nothing in response. Out of her past, the face of her only teacher surfaced, an Egyptian Ghaziya who never tired of reminding her that all belly dancers were gypsies to begin with, and gypsies they would always remain. She'd never forgotten and she'd never stopped wandering—until the day she found love. He was a tall strong man, with laughing eyes, surrounded by deep creases. She had left him for a year; then she'd returned to him. She had no illusions, but she was determined to stay by his side until the day she understood it was well and truly over.

A little further along the row of storefronts, she noticed a pair of shoes and made a mental note to come back some other time. Now she had to hurry home. On her day off, the evening and the night were consecrated to her lover.

A few steps short of her car she slipped her hand into her purse, rummaging for the remote. She heard a rustle behind her and out of the corner of her eye she saw the side door of a panel van slide open. Strong arms seized her and dragged her into the windowless van. For a split second her eyes darted around in the dark, desperately searching for the only person who could save her. But her love wasn't there. She wondered if she'd ever see him again.

With violent efficiency she was immobilized, gagged, and blindfolded. She'd spent enough time in nightclubs and she'd seen enough of the scum of the earth that tended to congregate in them to understand that they had no intention of killing her. Not right now, anyway.

She felt a sharp sting at the side of her neck. After a few seconds, a merciful lethargy coated the fear, numbing her.

The foreigner took a large gold ring out of his pocket and fastened it to the woman's keychain. Then he stepped out of the panel van, opened the door of the smaller car, and slid the keychain and ring under the front seat. To him the act was meaningless. It was a request of his client, who had paid a handsome bonus for that bizarre grace note.

He got behind the wheel of the panel van and started the engine.

A few hours later, when the town was already slumbering and the streets were deserted, a man opened the door of the woman's car. He ran a hand over the dashboard and peered between the seats in search of a clue, any evidence at all, that might tell him where she had gone. He'd waited for her to come home until there was no conceivable explanation for her absence, and then he set out to find her. When he found the ring under the seat his heart began racing, thumping. He suppressed an urge to roar in fury. It took him long minutes of effort to calm himself down; he sniffed the air inside the car. He could just barely detect the unmistakable scent of the perfume that the woman ordered from a small producer in Florence. Bad sign. It meant that whoever had taken her had several hours' head start.

* * *

That evening, I was in a bar in the center of Padua. It was one of those bars that serve spritz by the quart, with all the customers outside, plastic glasses in one hand and cigarettes in the other. The smoking ban, aside from making bars and nightclubs a little less festive and customers and waiters a little healthier, had also led to an invasion of the piazzas and sidewalks. In the city of Padua, more than a few citizens felt that this new fashion deserved public debate, motions and adjournments in the city council meetings, and rivers of ink in the pages of the local press. Even though the great recession was still looming on the horizon, the signs were clear that the country was going to the dogs. Wasting time and energy on pointless issues had already become a national sport.

The woman I'd arranged to meet rushed in. She was afraid she was late; she was, in fact, late—by a good ten minutes. Since she'd never met me, she had no idea how elastic I was when it came to punctuality. She looked around wildly, trying to figure out which of the people at the bar could be me. I waved a hand to help out.

"Are you Marco Buratti?" she asked, hesitantly.

I nodded. "Care for a drink?"

She shook her head. I shrugged and sipped my spritz. Prosecco, Campari, seltzer, a splash of Cynar, an orange slice, ice. That's how I drank it. There were countless variations, and by now even the Chinese knew them all—the Chinese had been buying up bars in Padua for years now.

I gave her a chance to give me the once-over while I lit a cigarette.

"All things considered, you look pretty sinister," was the opinion she came to. "Maybe I made a mistake when I agreed to meet you."

I smiled at her—it was a way of warning her not to act too snooty. I pointed at the cowboy boots sticking out of the legs of my blue jeans and ran my hand over my beat-up leather jacket. "You don't like my style?" I asked.

She tried a weak counterattack. "All the other private investigators have big half-page ads in the yellow pages and . . . you're not even listed."

"Well, as far as that goes, I don't even have a license."

She gasped in amazement, and her mouth remained open. "So you're going to try to blackmail me?"

I was done being patient. "What I'm trying to do is save your ass, gorgeous," I hissed at her in a brutal whisper. "Like I told you on the phone, your husband's lawyer hired me; your husband suspects that you're sleeping with his business partner."

"That's not true," she said, her voice rising to somewhere just short of a shriek.

"And I know that. In fact, you've been screwing a civil engineer you met at the gym."

"Have you told my husband?"

"No."

She let out the deepest sigh of relief of her thirty-nine years of life. "Are you going to?"

I pretended to give a solemn air to the occasion by lifting my glass to my lips. In fact, I had no intention of ratting her out.

There was a time when I would have. The client was sacred, but then one day it dawned on me that the universe of suspicious spouses deserves only to have its wallets emptied and that, all things considered, cheating on your husband or wife is just one of the many ways of making it through the day, or night. What really pounded the concept into my head was a blonde from Mestre, just outside Venice, who caught me following her one day. Her arguments and her tone were highly persuasive. "At work, my boss busts my chops, my daughter's going to have to wear her braces for another two years, and my husband is a regular guy, but I might have been a little overhasty when I decided he was the man of my dreams," she said practically without a pause. "So I step out on him occasionally; nothing serious, just a bout of pure sex, and then I feel better. Can you understand that?" I nodded and then shared a couple of tricks with her to keep the man to whom she'd sworn eternal fidelity from getting too suspicious.

I tossed my plastic glass into a trashcan. "Sometimes, people are just in a hurry to get caught so they can send their marriage to hell in a handbasket and start a new life. If that's what you're looking for, I can hand over a couple of photographs to the lawyer," I explained to the woman sitting across from me, acting as if I was an expert on couples and relationships, though anyone can tell you (and on more than one occasion they've told me) that I don't understand fuck all about women—and my friends tell me so, to my face, from time to time.

"But if you're interested in holding your marriage together, then be a little more careful, and don't rely on technology. Text messages, emails . . . it's all stuff that was invented to make sure people leave tracks, to make it easier to keep an eye on them."

"I don't want to leave my husband," she mumbled, practically in tears.

I pulled my cell phone out of my pocket and called the lawyer who had hired me. "The woman's on the level," I told him. "The business partner is sleeping with the Irish au pair who takes care of his kids. He likes them young."

"Thank you . . ." she added, working herself into an emotional state.

I stood up, shook her hand, wished her good luck, and left, drifting out into the crowd swilling aperitifs. I strode across a piazza and slipped into a narrow lane in the old Jewish ghetto. I stopped off at Alberto all'Anfora and downed a glass of bubbly prosecco. I listened to people talking about the latest rugby match, and then I went home.

Back in those days, I owned a bar myself. I had a partner, a fat man named Max, also known as Max la Memoria—Max the Memory. The bar was just outside of Padua, and it occupied the ground floor of an old farmhouse that, miraculously, no one had demolished to make room for another of the countless industrial sheds that blighted the landscape. My customers called it La Cuccia—the Dog's Bed—because it was comfortable and welcoming, you could listen to good music, and the shelves behind the bar were crowded with bottles of good liquor.

From the day the bar opened, it was run by Rudy Scanferla, a bartender I'd known practically all my life. He knew his job, he worked hard in exchange for a good salary—and he never forgot to give himself cost-of-living salary hikes, indexed to inflation.

Scrawled across a mirror in red were a couple of verses of *I Drink*, a song by the blues goddess Mary Gauthier.

Fish swim
Birds fly
Daddies yell
Mamas cry
Old men
Sit and think
I DRINK

This represented the institutional philosophy of the bar, and my clientele respected it to the letter. You could smoke at La Cuccia. We'd spent a little money on a decent HVAC system, but we weren't up to code, so every month we handed out rustling bundles of cash to the various city inspectors. Nowadays there is just no way to be fully in compliance; the only way to stay in business was to hand out a few under-the-counter payments. On the other side of the transaction, people were lining up to be inspectors and enforcers of regulations: it wasn't quite as profitable as going into politics, but it did guarantee a comfortable income.

I had to admit that the inspectors weren't putting the screws to us too bad; our place wasn't the kind of bar that took in a lot of cash. It was a nightspot for liquor-drinkers who like to listen to good jazz and blues, so it was hardly fashionable.

Max and I liked our little place, though. For years we'd been sitting in the same old chairs at the same scratched-up desk where we received our clients: people who needed the services of a pair of ex-cons who'd decided to become private investigators. Actually, I'd had the idea in the first place; my partner showed up later. Our destinies intertwined when I decided that I needed someone with a memory like a steel trap and an obsession with keeping files. Then we just seemed to stay in touch. I'd given him half the bar and one of the two apartments I'd built upstairs.

It wasn't just an impulsive gift to a friend, a gesture of innate generosity. I'd taken his girlfriend to bed, and later she died in my arms, riddled with bullet holes, murdered by gangsters from the Brenta Valley underworld. Just one of the many guilt complexes I seem to collect and can't bring myself to put out with the trash.

Actually, we weren't a couple, we were a threesome. The third was a smuggler and armed robber who was pushing sixty. I first met him in prison, when I saved his life. Later, he returned the favor so many times I couldn't count. His name was Beniamino Rossini, but we called him Old Rossini to distinguish him from his many brothers. He was a good guy to have as a friend. As an enemy, he was very bad news.

La Cuccia wasn't open for business until ten at night. I knocked on the fat man's door.

"I'll bet you've dropped by just in time for dinner," he grunted, pretending to be annoyed.

"I'd be happy with a grilled cheese sandwich," I said, to get his goat.

"Then you've come to the wrong place."

I followed him into the kitchen.

"Tonight, *bigoli con ragù d'anatra*," he informed me, seizing a wooden spoon and wielding it with culinary authority. Long, thick noodles with a duck ragu. "It's all strictly organic," he pointed out as he sampled the sauce.

One of my partner's many personal quirks was his extreme rigidity when it came to cuisine. He was very capable at the stove, even gifted when it came to pots and pans, but he never ventured beyond the bounds of our local regional cuisine, of which he was a scholar and impassioned connoisseur. I've never really given much of a damn about food, but the years pass, and you start to run out of new recipes.

Frankly, I was starting to wish his culinary horizons could make a stretch beyond the bounds of Northeast Italy.

He popped the cork on a bottle of red wine from the Colli Berici. We drank a glass as the pasta boiled.

"I've invited someone to dinner tomorrow night," he announced.

"I'll make sure to stay away," I reassured him, before asking: "Is she another Lacan-quoting shrink like the last three?"

"No, I seem to have run out of those," he answered, resentfully. "She's a substitute teacher, a militant member of the worker's collective, divorced, no kids."

"Cute?"

"Not only is she cute," he exulted. "She smokes, she drinks, she's not taking a creative writing course, and she doesn't have a gym membership."

"Sounds good," I noted, and felt an urgent need to change the subject.

My girlfriend Virna had dumped me. She told me that she was sick of complaining about the same things over and over, and that I'd never change. Then she'd thrown in a couple of observations that really stung. I hadn't seen her for months now, and I felt like a lonely loser. I was sad.

"The world is swarming with women. Numerically, they outnumber us men," was all that Max said—he'd always predicted that it would end badly with Virna.

The fact remained: I still wanted Virna. I was forty-seven years old, I had no intention of looking around for someone else or figuring out a dating strategy. At least, that's what I still thought that night. I didn't know that every aspect of my life was about to be turned upside-down. Fate had nothing to do with it. It was the past come back to settle a few old scores that we'd forgotten about. The past: it was going to rip through all our lives with the blind fury of a Force 12 hurricane.

Not a day has gone by since then that I don't think back to the instant, a few hours later, when the front door of La Cuccia swung open and Beniamino Rossini walked through it. I understood immediately that something was wrong, seriously wrong. His face was gray, his jaw was clenched, his gait was rigid. He let himself collapse into the chair next to me. Max la Memoria came over at the same time: he'd noticed the stricken expression on our friend's face too.

Rossini lifted his right fist till it covered his face, and then he smashed it violently down onto the tabletop. Heads swiveled the length of the bar and across the big room. Then he slowly turned the fist over and spread his fingers wide. Max and I exchanged a glance. We'd both immediately recognized the ring in his hand. And it was the last thing we'd ever expected to see.

"Where'd you find that?"

"In Sylvie's car," he whispered. "Under the front seat," he added.

I felt a chill run through my veins. In June of 2004, I'd left that same ring under the front seat of someone else's car. It was a death notice.

"What about Sylvie?"

"She's gone."

All three of us were sure she was dead. The man who'd once owned that ring was dead; he'd been murdered and buried next to a highway construction project. Putting the ring in the car was a funeral announcement to the man's gang. Those are the kind of courtesies gangsters used to extend to one another.

Max gulped down his grappa. "Why take it out on Sylvie?"

Rossini clicked his lighter and carefully moved the flame to the tip of his cigarette. "Maybe they just want to enjoy this. Maybe they started with her so we'd know they're planning to fuck us one after the other, and take their sweet time doing it."

"Maybe they just want to get back the body of the guy with the ring," the fat man shot back.

That made no sense. "Let's calm down," I mumbled. "We're just taking stabs in the dark here."

"You calm the fuck down," Rossini barked. "They just murdered my woman."

"We don't know that," I whispered uncertainly.

"I've spread the word that I'm trying to track down something very important," Beniamino told us. "There's not a drug smuggler working the land routes or the shipping lanes, not a dealer or a Mafioso of any nationality, who hasn't been told. What more can I do?"

Old Rossini was a beaten man; his voice was hoarse with tension. I pointed a finger at the ceiling to summon our new Pakistani waiter. I couldn't remember his name. Max had hired him; another in a long line of illegal immigrants, and at the end of the month we'd just have to pay a surcharge on our bribe, to keep from having him tossed out of the country. I told him to bring water and vodka for our friend.

A surreal silence settled over the table, until Beniamino broke in with a phrase that was heavy with truth. "I was crying on the way over here. I was sobbing like a baby . . . Until now, I made other people cry."

Yeah. We were at a loss. We'd always known exactly what the next move should be. But now we had no idea where to look for Sylvie, because the guy who once wore that ring was nobody, a total stranger to us all, and we'd never bothered to find out who he was. Beniamino had murdered him with a bullet to the head, because he'd tried to drag us into something we wanted no part of. It was self-defense, really. At the time, we were sure that there'd be no consequences. Nothing could have been further from the truth.

I lit a cigarette. It had a metallic taste. I rinsed my mouth with a slurp of Calvados. Rossini reached out and grabbed the pack of cigarettes. "Let's do something, because I'm about to lose my grip. I don't want to wreck this bar; I'm kind of fond of it."

We walked out of La Cuccia and into the cold late-October night, filling our lungs with fresh air, and got into Rossini's car. At the East Padua tollbooth, we passed a couple of Carabinieri squad cars. The cops would be the last to know about Sylvie's disappearance, if anybody ever decided to tell them—say, someone with a personal interest in doing so. This was underworld business: it was a mathematical certainty that it was going to end badly. No fucking judge, lawyer, or court could do anything to fix this. Somebody was going to die. That was the only thing we knew for sure as the car raced eastward in the night.

We searched for Sylvie for ten days. We looked everywhere. We turned Northeast Italy inside-out like a sock, we twisted arms and cracked knuckles, we interrogated everyone we thought might know something. Old Rossini was a wounded tiger. Whenever Max and I talked to someone, he stood quietly aside, but he was the one they looked at with worried eyes. To look at him was to feel fear. We stepped on toes, we tipped over apple carts, we went straight to the top. Our breaches of etiquette weren't making us popular.

One Bulgarian, who ran a prostitution ring and knew every way you could transport a woman across the border—entering Italy or leaving it, voluntarily or against her will—finally ran out of patience and openly insulted us. He told us to quit wasting his time. Beniamino came to see him in the middle of the night; he jammed the barrel of his pistol against the Bulgarian's forehead. He sat smoking a cigarette in silence, staring at the white wall of the bedroom. The white-slaver, certain he was about to be murdered, couldn't take it. He passed out and hit the floor with a thud. So Old Rossini got up to leave. It was only then that he noticed the terrified woman, motionless, under the feather quilt.

"Things can't go on like this," I said after a tense meal in a restaurant in Udine. "Much more and they'll start shooting at us."

"I like being shot at," Beniamino snapped.

"You've gone off your gimbals," I said softly. "And who wouldn't? What we have to decide now is whether we want to self-destruct or find out what really happened to Sylvie."

"I'm not sure I see what you're saying," Rossini snapped at me.

I chose my words cautiously. "I just don't think it makes sense to keep looking for her like this. She's not anywhere around here. Either she's dead or they've taken her somewhere else, far away."

"Marco has a point," Max broke in. "We have to go back to the guy with the ring, and start over from there. We have to figure out who he is—who he was—and, step by step, figure out who's behind this."

"If we do that, we're sitting ducks," Rossini objected.

I sighed. "We always have been. Before they took Sylvie, and ever since. If they'd wanted to kill us, they could have done it easily. Our anger wouldn't have stopped them."

"They have something else in mind," the fat man added.

Beniamino stared at me, thinking about what I'd said. "I'm tired," he admitted. "Give me a couple of days to recover."

We went back to Punta Sabbioni, where he had lived with his beloved, but he refused to set foot in that handsome empty villa. He asked us to take him down to the marina. He cast off the lines and revved the engines of the deep-sea speedboat that he used for his smuggling operations, and headed out to open waters. He was probably going to hole up in some inlet on the

Dalmatian coast, and recalculate his relationship to life. Then he'd come back—ready to take things to the limit.

"I'm hungry," the fat man announced. "Let's go get some seafood."

"Shouldn't we head back? We can be home in an hour, and we could just make a plate of pasta."

Max wagged his index finger at me for emphasis. "Each of us has a different way of letting off steam," he said. "Beniamino has his speedboat, you have your blues and your Calvados, and I have food. I'm a fat compulsive overeater, and now I want to fill my belly, in proportion to the grief and the pain in the ass that this whole episode has been causing me . . ."

I raised my hands in surrender. "Fine, fine. Do you know how intolerable you can be when you take that tone?"

He gave me a sly sidelong smile. "Yeah? And to think I've mellowed with age. You should have heard me when I was a slim young leader of the student movement."

Aperitif, antipasto, pasta, entrée, side dishes, dessert, espresso. It wasn't until we were sipping our grappas that Max decided that the time had come to untangle the threads of the events that had turned Sylvie into the target of a vendetta.

"It was a mistake to bury that guy before we could find out exactly who he was," he began.

"Old Rossini was a little too hot-tempered," I conceded. "Still, the guy clearly wanted to use us, fuck us, and then dump us."

"Do you have any idea of where we can start digging to figure out this mess?"

"I've thought about it," I admitted. "And I asked myself: How did he hear about us? Who gave him our names?"

"Your name," the fat guy corrected me. "I remember perfectly that the day he walked into La Cuccia, he asked for you. 'I'm looking for the Alligator.' That's exactly what he said."

Thursday, April 1, 2004

Max was right. The guy had asked for the Alligator. They'd called me that ever since my time at university, when I sang vocals in a group called the Old Red Alligators. I wound up in prison, the group fell apart, I lost my voice, but the name stuck with me, and the blues, in spite of everything, continued to exist.

Whenever I wondered if the blues had died forever, I'd call my favorite blues-jay, Edoardo "Catfish" Fassio, and he'd provide me with reassurance in the form of compilations of new blues musicians, some Italian, some not, and "a few kick-ass classics."

It was April Fool's Day, and ever since I'd gotten out of bed I'd been on the lookout for the idiotic pranks of Max la Memoria. Max likes to play tricks. I don't like to have tricks played on me. Given my thin skin, being the butt of a prank on the first of April would have made me lose my temper, I think.

But the guy who sat down at my table caught me by surprise—and sure enough, I lost my temper. The first thing I noticed was the huge gold ring on his left ring-finger. The flat part of the ring had an engraving that might, at first sight, have been a cross. He was about forty-five, with a lean physique, though it must have been a while since he worked out. Long black collar-length hair, dark Italian designer suit, French shirt.

"So you're the Alligator." He spoke perfect Italian, but he was certainly a foreigner. A quick glance at his shoes persuaded me I'd guessed right. I tried unsuccessfully to guess his accent.

"Did you hear what I said?" he went on, arrogantly.

I held up the glass I was nursing in one hand. "This is called an Alligator," I explained. "Seven parts Calvados, three parts Drambuie, plenty of crushed ice, and a slice of green apple to nibble on when you're done, to console yourself that the glass is empty. My friend Danilo Argiolas, owner of the Libarium in Cagliari, created it."

He smiled tolerantly. "Are you done with the bullshit?"

"I haven't even gotten started," I shot back, thinking to myself that the guy wasn't just your standard-issue asshole. Still, I couldn't quite tell from his face what he was. A cop, a made man, a hired gun, a member of the intelligence services—difficult to say. I figured it was best to keep playing stupid. That day, I nailed the part to perfection.

"From today on, you're working for me."

"Finally, some good news," I blurted out. "I was just sitting here feeling moody and wondering when my prince would come."

"Maybe you'd like a little kiss to wake you up?"

"Which fairytale are we in? I'm having trouble keeping track."

He shook his head. "I'm hiring you to investigate the narcotics heist at the Institute of Legal Medicine."

"You've come to the wrong place."

Same smile as before. He really didn't have a lot of variations on his theme. "You and the two guys you work with can just start talking to people, asking around, until you find out who took that pile of narcotics. You'll be well paid, of course."

He pulled out the usual envelope stuffed with cash from the inner pocket of his jacket and dropped it with a thump in the middle of the table. I glanced at it carelessly.

"I just told you that you came to the wrong place."

"I know all about you. You're the right man for the job."

"Then you must know that I don't mess around with drugs."

"This time you're going to make an exception."

"Why would I do that?"

"Because nobody turns down a good job," he replied. "Especially if the prospective client might turn nasty."

"Beat it!" I hissed.

"You don't believe me, do you?" he asked, disappointed.

"That's not it. The thing is this: I'm not going to work for you. Do you understand me?"

He stood up. "You'll hear from me again."

As he turned to go, I reminded him to take the envelope of cash on the table.

"Oh, there's no hurry," he said. "We'll see each other again soon."

I watched him leave. He didn't look back. He walked with a confident, loose gait. He was the most dangerous of all the desperadoes who had come out of the woodwork in the past few weeks, trying to hire me to track down the trove of narcotics stolen from a high-security, armor-plated storeroom in the cellar of the Department of Forensic Toxicology. The answer had been the same for all of them. I don't mess around with drugs. In any way, shape, or form. Every so often, I smoke a healthy, organic joint. That's all. The world of narcotics is rotten in every sense of the world. Staying clear of it was just common sense. In any case, from the newspaper accounts, that case smelled like bad, bad news.

In the hours between the night of March 16 and the early morning of March 17, someone entered the Institute, punched in the code to deactivate the alarm system connected to the armored door, which was wired to contact a private security service, and used a key to open the lock—which had been replaced just the previous week. Whoever it was then made off with fifty kilograms of heroin, cocaine, and various tablets, cap-sules, and pills, without even bothering to glance at 127 kilos of high-quality hashish.

The theft had generated dismay among the honest citizenry of the city of Padua.

Voices were raised to ask why such a huge quantity of narcotics was being stored at the Institute; after all, for the necessary legal testing, a few grams would have been more than sufficient. Was it possible that there was no safer place in the city?

As chance would have it, the solution was found immediately after the first two parliamentary inquiries; the decision was made to put into effect an "anti-temptation" protocol. From now on, the police would bring in a few grams of evidence to the Insitute of Legal Medicine to test for narcotics and the rest of the confiscated substance, after a few days, would be destroyed in the nearest incinerator.

Of course, the ensuing investigations turned up nothing. Of course—because anyone daring enough to use keypad codes and keys must be perfectly confident that their ass is completely covered, that the risk is nonexistent. There were police sweeps and distractions, midnight interrogations, adroit leaks of "possible arrests in the next few hours." All the usual things. But it was just so much hot air to fill the mouths of well-informed chatterboxes.

The secondary effect of the theft was, in fact, the arrival in Padua of a handful of desperadoes, as Rossini described them, embarking on a feverish treasure hunt for that trove of narcotics. The scum of the earth, dealers and smugglers who wanted to understand just what had happened, in hopes of getting their talons into that pile of drugs or else to arrange a deal with whoever had taken it: because if they couldn't get the narcotics, it was equally interesting to get in touch with anyone who had connections with powerful and corrupt insiders.

Northeast Italy was a profitable and flourishing market. The competition, however, was cutthroat. Everyone was playing dirty, at the many different tables. The favorite pastime was to sell out rival gangs to the unfortunate policemen, who were constantly struggling frantically, and pathetically, to track down something—anything. A simple chemical analysis of the local sewage revealed an endemic use of narcotics. Cocaine first and foremost. A snort of energy and excitement before and after work and, just for fun, on the weekend. Otherwise, what a drag it all was; what a chore.

In the back of my mind, I was hoping that the pain in the ass with the big gold ring would be the last desperado to come around busting my chops. I filed the incident away. I thought of it again a few hours later. About ten in the morning the next day, Ramzi, an illegal immigrant from Mali who worked as our janitor, kept knocking at my door until I finally got out of bed. He was a hard-working guy, still struggling to recover from the long journey that had brought him to our nice, welcoming little town. He was about fifty, and at that age it's crazy to undertake the dangers and discomforts of a trip of that kind. His experience had left him short of breath, with a wheeze that rattled from the depth of his lungs.

In his halting Italian, he managed to convey to me that, just outside La Cuccia's front door, there was something that I absolutely had to see. I threw a dressing gown over my pajamas and went downstairs to take a look.

"Would you do me a favor and go wake up Max?" I asked Ramzi as I stood looking down at a tangle of wires and a bundle of sticks of dynamite.

"If you ask me, it was the guy with the ring," I said to the fat man a few minutes later.

"Do you think it could blow up?" he asked in a sleepy voice. "I mean, in the sense that we might be a pair of assholes standing here looking at a bomb that's about to explode?"

"I have no idea," I replied. "But from the looks of it, it doesn't seem all that dangerous."

The illegal immigrant broke in. "No blasting cap," he said in French.

Max la Memoria translated and I asked Ramzi how he knew for sure. That's when we found out that Mali had an army.

"Call Old Rossini," the fat man recommended before heading back to bed.

The next turn of events was obvious enough. That same evening the guy with the ring came back to the bar. He made himself comfortable in the same chair. But this time I wasn't alone. Max was at my right, Rossini was at my left.

"The answer's still no," I said immediately.

He ignored what I'd just said. He gestured a greeting to my two friends, pulled out another envelope stuffed with cash, and pushed it slowly and deliberately to the center of the table.

"Dynamite and cash," the fat man commented. "Is that your clever way of convincing us to take your job?"

The guy nodded with satisfaction. "I'm kind of in a hurry," he explained to Beniamino. "I need results, and quickly."

The old smuggler sat in silence, and looked at the guy in an apparently offhand manner.

I pulled the first envelope out of the back pocket of my blue jeans and laid it on top of the second envelope. "Now leave, and don't come back."

"I wish I could, but I can't," he said, with a hint of feigned regret. "I don't like this bar, you guys don't like me, I don't really like you, but as you can imagine, orders are orders, and I don't give them, I take them. I can't go back without results."

"Then why don't you get busy and ask around?"

"I tried," he admitted with a sigh. "But I don't know anyone, and when I got back to my hotel, there was a plainclothes policeman who started asking rude questions. He wanted a thousand euros just to leave me alone."

"I tell you, you start to miss the cops we had in the old days," I commented as I lit a cigarette. "These days, the cops are all demanding and arrogant."

"Why can't you guys be reasonable?"

"Because we'd be of no use to you," Max replied in an accommodating tone. "It's not our area of expertise. We wouldn't be able to find out a thing."

"I was given assurances to the contrary."

"Well, those assurances were crap," my partner retorted.

The guy fiddled with his ring. It was the first time that I'd noticed him doing that. He must have been pretty upset. Then he waved his index finger jauntily in the air. "Oh well, it's not really that hard to find blasting caps . . ."

He might have been planning to finish the sentence but Rossini didn't give him a chance. He jumped to his feet, grabbed the bentwood chair he'd been sitting on, and broke it over the guy's back. The guy shouted in pain and took to his heels.

You could have cut the silence in the bar with a knife. The astonished, worried expressions of the customers were clear evidence that the incident hadn't passed unobserved.

Max stood up. "We beg your pardon," he began in a solemn voice, "but this was a simple disagreement between rivals in love. Nothing serious, we assure you."

A woman's voice piped up from the far side of the bar: "Hey Max, if you expect us to buy that big a lie you'd better pick up all our bar tabs."

I traded a glance with my partner. "Of course," he said loudly. "Consider it done. And the next round is on the house."

Amid the laughter and applause of the customers, I heard the same woman's voice: "You're a gentleman, Max. I guess we'll erase this incident from our memories, to try and save the good name of La Cuccia."

There was a general burst of laughter, and it proved contagious. We all laughed too. It's nice to laugh. It happens rarely enough. And yet I read somewhere that it's good for your health.

"Rivals in love . . ." Beniamino muttered indignantly. "Are you trying to make me look like a fool?"

"Couldn't you wait for him to leave the bar?" the fat man snapped back.

"Calm down, the two of you," I broke in. "Nothing happened, so let's just enjoy ourselves, for Christ's sake."

Beniamino looked hard at me. "You really think that asshole's done with us?"

"I sure hope he is. I really don't want to have to go sleep in a hotel just because he decides to plant some more of his homemade bombs."

The bastard didn't use explosives; all he needed was a tank of flammable liquid to completely destroy my 1994 Skoda Felicia, the first model year. Ramzi tried to console me by telling me that, first of all, it was an old car and, second, since I was a wealthy inhabitant of a developed nation, I could just buy myself a better fucking car.

I didn't waste time explaining that I was fond of my Felicia and that, statistically, that model of Skoda was the least likely to be stopped by the police at roadblocks and random checkpoints. That's not to say that I always had something to hide or be afraid of, but a quick computer check would always bring up my history as a convicted political criminal. That kind of background check was just the thing to make our jolly local cops, even more close-minded than our local priests, turn against you. Once a terrorist, always a terrorist, at least that's the way they saw it.

Though I'd never been a terrorist. I'd just provided a place to stay to a fugitive from the law, without asking too many questions. So they threw me into prison for seven long years.

I needed to find another Skoda Felicia in good condition. I figured I'd ask Paolino Valentini, a guitarist I knew who was as crazy about that model of car as I was—though for different reasons.

Rossini showed up around sunset. "I'm going to have kill

him," he mused as he stood looking at the charred remains of my Felicia.

"Do you really have to do it?"

"We were perfectly polite. Good manners aren't enough. If word gets around, there'll be people lining up to use us as doormats."

I tried to lock eyes with Max, but he just shrugged.

Another gold bracelet would join others dangling from Beniamino's wrist. Each of those bracelets is his way of brandishing a scalp. Or else of keeping count, I never was sure which. It always struck me as too touchy a subject to ask about openly.

I had my doubts. Serious doubts. "Let's just throw a scare into him and see how it goes."

The smuggler grimaced dubiously. "I don't think it'd work. Maybe he's too dumb to die."

The guy came back for the third night running. He walked up cautiously, his eyes on Old Rossini's hands.

I showed him the two envelopes full of cash. "My Felicia is worth these two plus another," I hissed furiously.

"No problem."

"We may have a lead," Max lied.

"I'm listening," the guy said, hopefully.

"First we need to know what you're really interested in. The drugs? The thieves? The mastermind?"

"I can't tell you that."

"You can't tell or you don't know?" I asked, provoking, suggesting he was just a hired thug.

"You just worry about finding out all you can. I'll worry about what interests me," he snapped peevishly.

"Well, that's not the way this thing works," the fat man put in. "We may, and I reiterate, we just may have found out where some of the heroin wound up. What we can do is take you to see the dealers who are selling it off, and then you can do what you want to fill in the blanks. That part's up to you."

"Okay. When can I meet them?"

"Tomorrow evening."

We arranged to meet just outside of Mestre, toward the airport, but before he left, I made sure he paid me a full refund on the loss of my car.

"He seems like a fake," I said as I counted the bills under the table.

"Why?" asked Rossini.

"He keeps pulling out envelopes full of cash, he knows how to get explosives and timers, he knows how to torch a car, but he still strikes me as a moron," I explained. "He just acts dumb. I have a problem believing that he swallowed the story we fed him tonight."

Rossini shrugged. "These days, you meet all kinds. Real professionals are few and far between. Anyway we'll find out soon enough. If he shows up, and if he shows up alone, then he's a real idiot."

"He might be, and his bosses might not."

"Yeah, well, they'll find out that it's a bad idea to keep bothering us."

The guy with the ring turned out to be a real amateur. He showed up, on time and without bodyguards, in an absolutely deserted part of the countryside, where bulldozers had just turned the landscape into a dusty plateau, where a section of superhighway overpass was going to be built, with pylons and on-ramps. Just another piece of the monumental infrastructure that the governor of the region was assembling so that posterity would remember him as an enlightened statesman.

The minute the guy stepped out of his car, Rossini had a pistol barrel pressed tightly against his forehead; he led the guy over to the brink of a deep ditch. It was roomy enough for two more corpses, just in case he'd decided to bring some muscle with him. That of course had been the farsighted Beniamino's idea. Neither Max nor I would have dreamed of going to the bother and the effort of shoveling out any more dirt than we were sure we would need: count the corpses, then dig the grave.

"This could be yours," the old smuggler whispered. "If you disappear, if you never show your face around here again, well, we might leave it empty."

In response, the guy just jammed his elbow hard into Beniamino's belly. Beniamino's trigger finger snapped down on the trigger. A bullet tore into the idiot's temple. He was dead before his knees hit the ground.

Rossini stood there gasping for a few seconds. "I've never seen anyone try so hard to get murdered."

The fact that we were sure we were dealing with a dangerous amateur lulled us into overconfidence. We didn't waste any time going through his pockets or rifling through the car. I drove his car all the way to Vicenza myself. Then, as a thoughtful gesture, we left the ring inside, so that his friends, bosses, or accomplices could be sure that he had been eliminated.

And that was it. The next day, we'd already forgotten it ever happened. No remorse. We'd done everything we could to drive it into his head that he'd picked the wrong people.

Of the three envelopes stuffed with cash, we used one to buy me a new Felicia. Unfortunately, I couldn't find a first year model and I had to settle for a 1996 Skoda Felicia. We used the second envelope to get Ramzi medical treatment and legal immigrant status. And we put the third envelope into the letterbox of an association devoted to rescuing and rehabilitating streetwalkers. Most prostitutes are victims of the white slave trade, and they live in an atmosphere of terror and incessant violence. We had an abiding respect and admiration for the volunteers who went out every night to try to persuade prostitutes to break free.

The months that followed were untroubled. The only big news in the year 2004 was the fact that Sylvie came home in early December. We celebrated at La Cuccia. She danced for us, and it was an unforgettable night. Old Rossini was the happiest man on earth.

He whispered: "She showed up at my door, and said: 'I've come home to my bandit.'" Overcome with emotion, he wrapped his arms around me.

Max la Memoria walked into my apartment without knocking, wrapped in a garishly colored dressing gown.

He had a light-green file folder under one arm. "Nothing adds up in this narcotics heist," he said flatly. "Even the amount and the types of narcotics keep changing."

"What do you mean?"

"At first, they reported that forty-four kilos of narcotics was missing from the storeroom: thirty kilos of heroin, ten kilos of coke, and four kilos of amphetamines, ecstasy, and other assorted pills. But I found a written response from the deputy minister for internal affairs to a parliamentary inquiry in June 2004; there it says that forty-nine kilos of heroin were stolen, along with six kilos of coke and another couple of kilos of hash."

"That's a discrepancy of something like thirteen kilos. That's a lot," I commented, tossing a cigarette butt into the fireplace.

The fat man flopped onto the couch. "You want to know what I think?"

"I do," I answered. "You haven't come out of your study for the past two days."

He ran his fingers through his unkempt hair. "The thieves wanted the heroin."

"Someone hired them to do it. They had the contacts to move the product and they reached out and found someone willing to help them get inside."

Max handed me a newspaper clipping. "I'm not convinced that this job was about selling drugs."

I started skimming the article. The headline read: "Evidence Stolen, Acquittal in View?" I glanced at the date: July 3, 2004.

"They may be guilty, but there's a good chance the defendants will go free anyway. That's the unlikely outcome of the trial for the spectacular heist of narcotics from the Institute of Legal Medicine. There is a risk that the people who were peddling those narcotics will be acquitted and released . . . The district attorney's office is willing to negotiate a plea bargain, but according to reports from well-informed sources, the lawyers of those charged are opting for an abbreviated trial. No appeals. All or nothing . . ."

"Usually the couriers are just mules, and they cut them loose if they get caught," I answered, doubtfully. "I've never heard of a drug cartel putting together such a complicated plan to get a low-level transporter out of trouble."

"Maybe they weren't so 'low-level,' or maybe there's something else going on here."

"That may be. But I don't see how any of this can help us identify the guy with the ring and find out what happened to Sylvie."

When I said her name, I felt my stomach seize up, the way it always did in those days and weeks. The mystery shrouding her fate lured my mind toward territories infested with impossibly violent nightmares. A beautiful woman, a vendetta . . . there were all the ingredients, and I couldn't keep from thinking ugly thoughts.

"You're not listening," the fat man admonished me.

"Sorry, I just can't help thinking—"

Max held up a hand to silence me. "Let's make a deal, Marco: let's pretend this is just another case, or we're not going to be able to hold it together. And we've got to stay on track, we can't afford to lose it."

I nodded in agreement, and told him to go on.

"Finding out what really happened with the burglary, which might seem to have nothing to do with this, is crucial. We have to look into everything so we can figure out what role the dead guy played. I did some research on the ring. It's what's known as a *chevalier*, a signet ring. The flat part on top is where you would normally have an engraved coat of arms."

"An aristocrat?"

"I don't think so, that cross thingie was pretty crude, and I couldn't find anything like it in any of the heraldry sites I searched online," he said. "It definitely doesn't belong to any well known family."

"What else?"

My partner held out a pair of empty hands. "That's all I've got so far."

I looked over at the bottle of Roger Groult "Vénérable" Calvados and then over at the clock on the wall. It was 4:20 in the afternoon. I sighed. I still had a long time to wait before I could slurp down my first glass. For the past two years now I'd made a rule that I could only drink after dinner. It was the only way I could think of to avoid becoming an alcoholic. But every blessed day I did nothing but check the progress of the hands of the clock.

Max caught my gaze and smiled. "How I understand you," he said in a tone of complicity. "That's why I'm so careful not to slip into the quagmire of dieting. I'd just spend the day counting the minutes, terrified of turning into an anorexic."

I pointed to the bottle of grappa. "Drink a shot to my health and stop spouting nonsense."

"For a friend, it's the least I could do."

"Last night . . ." I started to tell him.

"As you sat watching the usual fucking television shopping show . . ." he mocked me.

"It relaxes me, you know that . . ."

"And between a mattress and a set of new pots and pans . . ."

"I remembered that the guy told us that before coming to see me he'd tried to do some looking around on his own, and he'd run into a cop who scalped him for a sizable wad of euros just to leave him alone."

"Yeah, I remember."

"So if that's true, it means that when the guy first came to town he had no idea of who we were."

Max finally got it. "Which means that it was the cop who gave him your name."

"Exactly."

"That is, unless he just made that part up . . ."

"Look, it's a lead, and it's worth looking into."

"I agree. Let's wait for Rossini."

"He's on his way. He called about half an hour ago."

Beniamino's face was hollowed out, his eyes sunken with tension. He was impeccable as ever, shaven, sweet-smelling, and neatly dressed, but pain was carving an abyss deep inside him.

We were friends, so I didn't waste time. I told him what I thought: "The past few days on the Dalmatian coast haven't done you a lot of good."

He shook his head. "I'm just holding it together," he admitted. "And for the first time I've got ugly thoughts buzzing around in my brain."

I knew exactly what he meant. Find out the truth, take revenge, and put an end to it all. I didn't say anything. All things considered, I saw his point. How the fuck do you go on living with something so grim and tragic in your gut? For an instant, I thought how lucky I was this hadn't happened to me.

"That's right," I exclaimed aloud. "Why didn't it happen to me?"

The two others glanced at me quizzically.

"Why did they single out Beniamino? Why didn't they take Virna?"

"Maybe because she left you," Max suggested.

Rossini took off his camelhair overcoat. "No. It's because they know that of the three of us I'm the one that does murders. So I was the one they wanted to punish first."

"That's what I think," I said. "But that means that someone around here has been giving them information. And I think it has to be the same cop that gave my name to the guy with the ring in the first place."

"What cop?" the smuggler asked. I explained my theory to him.

"Then we have to try to find him," he concluded.

"We're going to need some cash," the fat man pointed out.

Beniamino pointed to the suitcase he was carrying. "I smashed my piggybank," he announced. "We can go."

We climbed aboard a large expensive French four-door, no longer in production. Rossini had held on to it because in the engine compartment there was a space that seemed to have been designed specially to conceal a pair of handguns. The guns were souvenirs of Beniamino's recent trip to the former Yugoslavia: brand-new, never fired, and if the police got hold of them, the guns would tell them nothing.

We started making the rounds of police informers. We handed out crips wads of bills in exchange for reports on the policemen who paid them.

"Unusual request," commented Raschio, a former heroin addict who worked the downtown piazzas, mingling with the spritz-sipping crowd to identify and report: not so much the dealers as the regular users. His specialty was screwing the little hipsters who sniffed smack: once they were caught in his web, in order to avoid further problems and to save their reputations and careers, they would in turn become informers. That was how the war on drugs worked.

His nickname, Raschio, was Italian for "rasp," and it came from his voice, which resembled a metal file grinding down a piece of rebar. "Maybe my own cop might be interested to know about this," he added in a sly tone of voice.

"We're looking for one in particular to do a piece of business," I explained in a conciliatory tone of voice. "When we do find him, if he hears that you've been causing trouble, he might just lose his temper."

Raschio thought about it for a minute and decided that he'd settle for a payment from us alone. He knew Rossini's reputation, and even if Raschio was no smarter than the average informer, he did understand that it was to his advantage not to run the risk of pissing off the old smuggler.

"Guys, there's a damned army of them," the fat man said late that evening, with a tone of exasperation. "It's a good thing we're only working the narcotics informers."

" . . . and we're limiting ourselves to the ones who were operating in 2004," I pointed out.

"I'm sick of meeting pieces of shit and giving them money—my money," Rossini threw in, angrily. "Let's get a pizza and go to sleep. We'll start again tomorrow."

I still hadn't had a drop of liquor. I was looking forward to the triple ration I would savor later on, stretched out on the sofa by the fireplace.

The next day, Old Rossini showed up a little before noon. "Let's go have an aperitif with the stool pigeons."

There were informers of every kind, sex, and nationality. The world of tipsters and stool pigeons is intricate and variegated. Every one of them has a different personal story, and in many cases it's not extortion that's driving them to betray their fellow man. For some of them, it's like a calling. They're good at it. Take the case of Morena Borromeo. She had tried working in a number of legal venues, but nothing worked out. She was very attractive, she knew how to dress, and she had started frequenting the best places in town. After a succession of failed relationships with the sons of wealthy businessmen, she started sniffing cocaine and turning the occasional discreet trick. Occasional, carefully considered, and well paid. Nonetheless, she found herself in trouble with the law. Luckily for her, a compassionate cop with nice manners pointed out an alternative, explaining that she knew lots of things, valuable information that could be worth cold hard cash on the right market.

And so she became a professional informant. She was good at her job—she had an uncanny gift for getting people to spill the beans. Especially men. It's the oldest story in the world: men talk in bed. And lowlifes talk more than anyone else. Maybe not about themselves, but in order to look smart, they will tell other people's secrets. And she was there, ready to accept, sort, and merchandise that information.

I knew her very well. She'd once dated a small-town industrialist who had made his fortune by manufacturing bicycle wheels. Then, when the market was ripe, he made his move and shifted his operation to Romania, because paying taxes to the corrupt national government in Rome and negotiating with the powerful Italian trade unions had become a pain in the neck. The fool thought he was sleeping with a lady. One day he confessed that he was sick and tired of the underage girl he'd been screwing in Timişoara. As Morena was slipping on her panties, she told him that she'd be needing an extra chunk of cash, or her conscience would drive her to report him to the police and tell everything to his wife.

The man turned to a lawyer, who hired me to do the negotiating. At first, I refused to have anything to do with it. It struck me as a classic case of sexual exploitation with side dishes of bullying and cash. But the industrialist insisted on having a meeting with me at any cost. He swore that he would leave the sixteen-year-old Romanian girl alone; in fact, he would give her a job and provide her family with assistance.

The lawyer vouched for the man's promise. I agreed to take the job; it was the only way I could see that the girl might come out of this with anything more than a kick in the ass. But making a deal with Morena proved to be somewhat more complicated. She played the part of the society lady, she made appointments to meet in expensive restaurants, and she named a stratospheric sum. I managed to wrestle her down to fifty thousand euros, to the enormous relief of the victim of her extortion.

Then I happened to run into her occasionally in the places people went for an aperitif. She greeted me jubilantly, as if we were old friends. I had always preserved a professional attitude with her, courteous and slightly distant, but deep down I kind of liked her. I liked her enough to wind up in bed with her. One night I shared my feelings with my friends, hoping they would give me a little encouragement. It was a mistake.

"How can you even think of it?" Max admonished me. "She's the spitting image of the evil stepmother from Snow White."

"There's nothing our Marco likes better than a dangerous slut," Beniamino said in an oracular tone. "Like that time in Sardinia that he went to bed with a psychopathic killer."

"I remember her well. The notorious Gina Manes," the fat man recalled.

"Let's not delve into the past," I protested.

"Fair enough. But you don't know shit about women," Old Rossini concluded tersely. We changed the subject.

But the day I saw her again, perched on a barstool, her legs crossed to good effect, dressed elegantly in a short-skirted but expensive suit, I regretted not having at least given it a shot with her. If I hadn't been so upset over Sylvie's kidnapping, I would have offered to buy her a drink.

Morena didn't miss my appraising glance. "Are you here on business or pleasure?"

"Business."

"But you wouldn't mind taking a little time off from your business, would you?"

"Nothing doing."

She grimaced like a naughty little girl making a face. "Liar."

Morena wanted to keep playing games. The sight of my two friends, however, made it clear that the time had come to start negotiating.

"I have a lot of gifts to hand out at Christmas," she announced. "I am very expensive this time of year."

"Shut up and listen," Rossini whispered.

"Oh my, your friend's quite the gentleman," she commented as she got down from her stool. She took my arm and pointed to a table off in a quiet corner. "I'm going to talk to you and no one else."

I explained to her the kind of information we were looking for. Her cocaine-reddened nostrils flared, like a she-wolf who senses her prey.

"How much is in it for me?"

"Don't work yourself into a frenzy," I told her in a flat voice. "This is a small deal."

She plunged her red-enameled fingernails into her glass and pulled out the orange slice. She sucked it reflectively to let me see how good she was. "I don't believe you."

"Well, that's your mistake."

"As far as the police are concerned, the investigation into the narcotics heist is a closed case," she explained. "If this evening I called up my handsome policeman who pays me a monthly salary and told him that I can detail the names of those responsible, he wouldn't even bother coming by."

That was interesting. "Why not?"

She made the gesture of clapping a cover onto a pot. "I just told you: case closed."

"Looks like you know plenty about it."

She smiled. This time, she wasn't seductive at all. "Maybe. But if I find out anything, I want ten thousand euros."

"You just priced yourself out of the market," I said as I got to my feet.

She grabbed me by the wrist. "My handsome policeman was involved in the investigation, but not officially, you understand?"

I understood perfectly, but it wasn't in my interest to act too interested. "Like a lot of people in that period."

She got up and brought her lips close to my ear. "But he likes two things," she whispered. "Money, and the way I suck his cock."

Her warm breath sent a shiver down my back. "The number of my cell phone is still the same," I muttered as I walked off.

Late that afternoon, Old Rossini lost his patience with an asshole who had served a long prison sentence for kidnapping and was trying to rip us off. The guy must have forgotten that all three of us had been guests of the state, and that we knew every angle to the art of lying. We were in a pub, and the guy was sitting next to Beniamino. The smuggler did nothing more than to reach down his hand and grab the guy's testicles, crushing them with a grip that had made him legendary in the underworld.

The asshole gasped, his mouth wide open in atrocious pain, unable to emit even the smallest sound, and keeled forward until his forehead rested on the table. "Fuck. You," hissed Rossini.

"Let him be," I said, worried that someone might notice what was happening. "Prison wasn't good for him."

"Why? Do you know someone that prison was good for?" Max retorted in an argumentative tone.

"It was just a way of saying his brain is fried."

The fat man wouldn't drop the bone. "Beniamino has spent more time in prison than this jerk," he insisted. "So what? Are you saying his brain is fried more than this asshole sitting next to us?"

The former kidnapper leaned toward the wall and vomited. We barely noticed.

"What's wrong with you?" I asked. "You trying to start an argument?"

The fat man denied it. "The fact is that sometimes you just talk nonsense. Around this table, all told, is more than forty years of prison, and you start making jokes."

Old Rossini stood up. "That's enough," he ordered. Then, to Max: "Ask the next shrink that you take to bed if she'll be so kind as to help you get over your prison complex. You haven't served enough time to justify these poses as if you were a lifer."

The fat man was about to deliver a comeback when the waiter arrived. Eastern European accent. Ukrainian, maybe. He pointed at the guy bent over double on the bench and the remains of his lunch on the floor.

"Who's going to clean that up?" he demanded, in disgust.

"The fact is that the beer you serve here is too cold," I complained.

"And watered down," Beniamino threw in.

As we walked past him, I slipped a twenty euro note into the breast pocket of his shirt. "Sorry about that."

Every so often I got into a fight with Max. That happened less frequently with Beniamino and when it did, we got over it in ten minutes. Max la Memoria, in contrast, held a grudge longer than I did, and sometimes days and days would go by before one of the two of us would make a gesture of reconciliation.

This time, the situation was different, and I wasted no time. "From now on, I'll try to avoid making references to prison."

Max burst out laughing. "Christ, that was fast! You didn't even give me time to sulk."

When we got in the car, I peeked into the rearview mirror

and saw the fat man looking out the window in a reverie. Beni-amino's words had hit hard, but he was right with a vengeance. Prison is a grim experience, and if you've ever been there, you have to deal with the aftermath sooner or later. Crying into your beer every chance you get does no good at all.

That night we drove the streets and roads, looking for old streetwalkers and transsexuals with reputations as informers. We only found one or two. The rest were retired now.

"Oh, the good old days are over," lamented Angelica, a transsexual who couldn't wear too short a miniskirt because of the equipment that dangled between her legs. "It's all foreign merchandise these days."

"Haven't you had your operation yet?" asked Rossini.

"I wouldn't dream of it. I'd lose all my clients," she shot back decisively. "You little men want us active and passive at the same time."

She was a straight dealer, and she made it very clear right away that there was nothing that she could do to help us. She'd settled her accounts with the cop that was blackmailing her, and now she made a living and was very careful to mind her own business. She refused the money I offered her for her trouble.

"It's too cold to stay out here on the street and I'm hungry," she said. "Why don't you come get a bite with me?"

We invited her to get in the car and we went to get a plate of spaghetti at a little place just outside of the city.

We got back to La Cuccia just before closing time. Rossini dropped us off at the front door and headed back to Punta Sab-bioni. I'd offered him a couch to sleep on at my place, but like every other evening he thanked me and refused, in case Sylvie reemerged from the darkness that had swallowed her up. He didn't say it in so many words, but that was clearly what he was thinking.

When we walked into the bar the first thing I noticed was that Rudy Scanferla was behind the bar, intently drying glasses, alone, with a grim expression on his face. It didn't take long to figure out why. There were two guys sitting at our usual table. I traded a quick glance with my partner.

"Cops," he whispered.

Old timers. White hair, faces with all the marks left by years of night shifts and early wakeup calls. Days punctuated by coffee and cigarettes. One of the pair waved us over. He had an immaculately trimmed snow-white goatee.

He came straight to the point. "You've been asking a lot of people a lot of questions. Now we want to know why."

"Did the top brass send you, or is this a personal initiative?" I asked.

"Buratti, don't be an asshole, answer my partner's question," the other cop cut in.

"I don't have anything to tell your partner."

"You know how tough we can make life for you."

I looked over at the fat man. Now it was his turn. "There's a lawyer who thinks that . . ."

"Shut up!" I shouted.

"No, you shut up!" the cop with the goatee snapped at me.

"As I was saying," Max went on, "there's a lawyer who hired us because he has a client who claims that he knows who did the burglary at the Institute of Legal Medicine. But before he takes him into court, he wants to make sure he doesn't wind up looking like an asshole."

"And just who is this drug dealer?" the other cop asked.

Oh, the fat man was good . . . My partner trotted out the first and last name of a Turkish courier who'd been arrested a few months earlier with five kilos of heroin. The two cops eased up visibly.

"That's crap," the cop with the white goatee declared, stroking his whiskers with one hand.

He took a pause to light a cigarette and then resumed his attack. "But you guys are looking for one specific cop, aren't you?"

"The Turk said that he's the mole," the fat man tossed out.

A smile of satisfaction glimmered briefly on the lips of both cops. Now they were sure that we were lost in the weeds. They got to their feet.

"Forget about this business," the cop with the white goatee said threateningly. "And that's not advice. It's an order."

They left the bar without closing the door behind them.

"They came in around halfway through the evening," said Rudy, coming out from behind the bar to go shut the front door. "They just took seats at your table without ordering anything and sat there, glaring at the customers. In less than twenty minutes, the place was empty."

"Don't worry about it. They're not coming back."

"Well, who do you think they were?" I asked my partner. "Carabinieri, treasury, state police?"

"I really don't know. I've never seen them before, and that's already a piece of information."

"Yeah, me neither. And I thought I knew every old-school cop around."

For thirty-six hours nothing happened. Rossini called every so often to find out if there was news; his tone of voice clearly betrayed a mounting tension and distress.

I was listening to the nasal voice of Percy Mayfield singing *You Don't Exist No More* when the ring tone of my cell phone cut through the notes of the blues.

"Ten grand—take it or leave it," Morena blurted over the phone.

I snapped the phone shut in her face. We were certainly willing to spend any amount of money to find out something—anything—about what had happened to Sylvie, but I knew Morena far too well. If I didn't hold up my end of the negotiating process in a respectable manner, she'd feel free to name any sum that came into her mind.

She called back ten minutes later. "I found the cop you're looking for."

"That makes you the seventh person just today," I lied.

"But I'm the only one who has the right name."

"At that price, no deal."

"I told you I wasn't cheap."

"Call me back when you land on planet Earth."

"Don't hang up on me . . ."

"Why, do we have something else to talk about?"

"We could talk about whether we do or don't over dinner."

A restaurant for cokeheads. The cooking was barely passable, the interior was discreet, elegant, and decorated like a box of bonbons; the clientele was made up of ambitious social climbers, male and female, who'd probably all had a few lines before dinner. I knew the owner. He'd spent a few years in prison for dealing drugs. Then he'd decided to get smart; he'd started the restaurant so he could peddle drugs in blessed peace. No one busted his chops because he paid the right people on time. He didn't even have to provide information; he just handed over three envelopes stuffed with cash to three different uniforms who came in to pick them up at regular intervals. Of course, among the customers were quite a few names that counted in Padua. As I walked in I noticed a couple of tables where more-or-less legal negotiations were being concluded, another three or four tables with illicit couples enjoying their dinners, and last of all, her, the queen of informers, looking at me with a smile.

"Have I ever told you how badly you dress?" she asked as I sat down at her table.

"More than once."

"You really look like an illegal immigrant, from one of the eastern bloc countries . . ."

"Once you told me that I dressed like an African."

"You were wearing a purple silk shirt, darling . . ."

She was dressed to turn heads, and heads were turning. I looked at her with frank appreciation, laying on a series of open expressions of lust that made her laugh with gusto.

"If I reached out under the table I bet I'd find something very hard to the touch," she said mischievously.

"A well-bred lady like yourself would never do anything of the sort."

Another laugh. The waitress came over with the menus. She was a mulatta. Almost certainly Cuban. She was cute and curvaceous, as required by the style of the restaurant. When we ordered, Morena demanded that the proprietor choose the wine. And of course an expensive bottle was brought to the table, the usual wine "constructed" by some fashionable enologist or other, with a pointlessly high proof.

After a while I got bored with staring at her tits, placed on generous display by her plunging neckline. "Well?"

"I know the name of the cop who sold your name to the guy who was looking for information about the burglary."

The time had come to find out whether Morena was telling the truth. "There's just one thing I don't understand," I said in a thoughtful tone of voice. "If the cops wanted to whitewash the case in a hurry, why suggest the name of the one private investigator who might be able to find something out?"

"Maybe because he knew that you don't get mixed up with drugs and his real objective was to get you in trouble."

I looked up sharply from my food. She really did know who it was. I cocked my head to one side. "Ten thousand, take it or leave it," she reiterated in a sugary sweet little voice.

"I'll take it."

She raised her glass. "Let's drink to our agreement."

"Tell me the name."

"Did you bring the money with you?"

I slapped my chest with my right hand, over my heart. "It's right here."

"We'll do this my way," she announced. "We're going to finish dinner, then you take me home and, far from spying eyes, we'll make the trade."

"Don't you trust me?"

"That's not it. It's that I like having you by the balls." When she saw the irritated expression on my face, she added: "Oh come on, let me have my fun for once."

As always, when you're in a burning hurry, the service was painfully slow. Morena got up twice to go snort a line of coke in a closet positioned strategically between the doors of the men's and women's toilets. The proprietor's wife took care of setting up the lines and providing disposable short plastic straws, though some customers brought their own straws, made of silver. The luxuries indulged in by people the police can't touch.

I finally succeeded in paying the check and dragging my informer out of the restaurant. She shrieked in horror at the sight of my Skoda Felicia.

"Why don't you buy a new car?" she wailed.

"Because I like this one," I replied brusquely. "If you prefer, I can call you a cab."

Morena lived in the center of town, in a big apartment building that might have been nice in the Sixties, but was now a horror to behold. She pulled a remote out of her purse and buzzed open the door to the underground garage. "No one will bother us down there."

I stopped my car in front of the private parking garage marked '7'. Morena unzipped my down parka, slipped a hand into the inside breast pocket of my blazer, and felt the envelope full of cash. After caressing my chest, she reached out, seized my chin, and kissed me.

"I'm in kind of a hurry to get that name," I said politely.

She started unfastening the belt on my trousers. "You really never listen. This time we're doing it my way."

I gave in. And it wasn't very difficult. "This isn't the most comfortable place," was my sole objection.

She opened the door of the car and got out, rummaging through her purse for the keys to the garage. A few seconds later, we were embracing in the dark. When she turned around and placed both hands on the wall and spread her legs wide, I hiked up her skirt and ran both my hands over her firm smooth ass. Then I lowered her panties to her ankles.

"Hurry up, Alligator," she urged. "I'm giving you a special price: just five hundred euros."

I stopped cold and she burst out laughing. "I'm joking, darling." She reached around, seized my cock, and guided it inside her. "Go slow," she said. "I want to enjoy this."

Beniamino and Max were waiting impatiently in my apartment. I'd called them the minute I left Morena's garage, after swearing to myself that I would never breathe a word about fucking her.

"De Angelis," I hissed the minute I set foot in the living room. "Arnaldo De Angelis."

"Wasn't he the cop that was implicated in that perjury case?" asked the fat man, true to his moniker. "When was it, 1998?"

"No, 1999," I corrected him.

De Angelis was a police detective who had decided to accuse an ex-convict of assaulting him in a deserted parking structure, fabricating the details out of whole cloth. Two shoves and a back-handed smack across the face that would have placed the defendant at a suspicious time and location, allowing the detective to shoehorn him into a much more serious set of charges: receiving and fencing stolen goods. This charming little set-piece was worth five solid years in terms of prison time. And since the detective needed a witness to prop up his fabrication, he asked a fellow cop to swear a false affidavit. I had been hired by the ex-convict's defense team, and I had little trouble discovering that the other cop had been out grocery shopping in a supermarket with his wife and kids.

I wanted to defuse things amicably, so I waited for De Angelis at his usual bar and showed him a photograph of his friend pushing a shopping cart down the frozen foods aisle, taken from the security camera feed, with a nice time stamp in the corner. The detective dropped charges, the defense lawyer got his client acquitted on the stolen merchandise rap. But evidently De Angelis still had it in for me, and he'd been patiently waiting for the first opportunity to pay me back: it took five full years for that opportunity to roll around. Patience and determination. Those are typical qualities of old school cops. He had retired about a year ago, Morena told me. She gave me his current address, too.

It was an expensive apartment building in a park-like setting just outside of town. Ten minutes by bike from the center of Padua. But the retired detective liked to walk. Actually he liked to run. The following morning, despite the biting chill in the air, we saw him emerge at eight sharp and trot away down the tree-lined lanes of his elegant neighborhood, dressed in a designer track suit. Precisely half an hour of aerobic exercise later, he made a quick stop at the newsstand and stepped into the café. We decided that I'd confront him, alone, as he stepped out of the café.

I materialized at his elbow. He recognized me immediately but continued walking. "Expensive neighborhood, top-floor apartment, doorman building," I greeted him in a cheerful voice. "Life is good on a detective's retirement plan."

He looked younger. He was fit and still a pretty good-looking man. He was tall with a handsome face and a full head of dark brown hair. Maybe some of that dark brown hair color was chemically enhanced, but at least he'd had the good taste not to dye it the strange Doberman pattern that so many Italian politicians seemed to be favoring lately.

He looked around cautiously. "What do you want, Buratti?"

"One evening, a couple of years ago, you extorted cash from a guy, a foreigner, who was asking around about the theft of narcotics from the Institute of Legal Medicine."

He lengthened his stride. "Leave me alone."

I hurried past him and wheeled around to block his path. "And you gave him my name," I went on. "He came to my bar and when I told him that I wouldn't work for him, he started acting tough, because that's what you told him to do, right?"

He threw up his hands. "I wanted to have a little fun with you. So?" he snapped. "You made me look like an asshole that time, and I just thought I'd return the favor. So I sent you that jerk. And now, two years later, you come busting my chops about it?"

"I just want to know who that guy is."

"I don't know who he is."

"Wrong. You'd never have pulled those moves with a total stranger."

He tried acting menacing. "I can still cause you a world of trouble."

"Yeah, so can I," I shot back. "Or else, in two minutes, you can be rid of me forever."

He puffed his cheeks in annoyance. "You have no idea how much I dislike you, Buratti."

"Well, you're not the love of my life either."

"He's Swiss," the retired detective began. "He's a lone operator, but one report said that he was an informer for the Serbian police."

Another spy. "What do the Serbs have to do with the stolen narcotics?"

"You've got me there. I have no idea," he muttered as he resumed walking toward his apartment building.

"And you never felt curious enough to try to find out?"

"No. Even if I had, I could never have tracked him down.

We don't have very good relations with those people, you know."

The Serbs, the meanest, toughest survivors of the former Yugoslavia. All the others were sugar candies in comparison. "What's his name?" I practically shouted. "What was he called?"

De Angelis couldn't remember, but he suggested that I go rummage through the old registers of a certain hotel.

"Look for a couple."

"He wasn't alone?"

"No. There was a woman with him. A nice piece of ass."

We waited till that night. Hotel desk clerks on the night shift tend to be much more tractable, and the empty lobbies help to lead them into temptation. They were painful hours. My friends made me repeat my conversation with the retired detective over and over again, dissecting it word by word. The involvement of the Belgrade police promised nothing good. It just made the whole story look more tangled than before.

At two in the morning I rang the hotel's front door intercom. A thirty-five-year-old Maghrebi buzzed me in. He wasn't very happy that I'd roused him at that hour.

"We don't have any vacancies," he said. "I'm sorry."

"I'm not looking for a room," I explained. "I'd like to talk to you."

He nodded resignedly. "Everyone wants to talk to me, and it's always at two in the morning," he complained. "Carabinieri want information about certain guests, whores want to bring customers into their room without registering names, drug dealers want me to take bags up to rooms . . . What do you want?"

"I want to check an old register."

"How much you willing to pay?"

I pulled out a 200 euro note.

He sighed. "I make 700 euros a month."

"Then this will come in handy."

"No question about it," he said as he took the banknote from my fingers. "Come in, follow me."

Half an hour later I left the hotel, turning to shake hands with the desk clerk at the door. I shivered as I walked out into the chilly air of that November night. I lit a cigarette and glared into the headlights of Beniamino's car; he had pulled away from the sidewalk and was moving slowly forward.

"His name was Pierre Allain, the woman was Greta Gardner," I announced as I handed Max the xeroxes of the two passports.

"Names that smell fake a mile away," the fat man snapped. "How the fuck can someone be named Greta Gardner?"

My partner's instincts were sound as usual. The passports were fakes. Another blind alley. Wasted money, precious time gone forever, and Sylvie further and further away. After another forty-eight hours of trying to find any clue or lead, we were forced to give up in despair. It had been exactly twenty-one days since she'd been kidnapped.

"Now what do I do?" Rossini wondered aloud. "Do I go home and tell myself, 'Tomorrow's another day,' or some such bullshit?"

Max and I stood there wordlessly. Just then, there was nothing anyone could have said. Beniamino left without saying goodbye. The fat man stood up and poured himself a healthy dollop of grappa.

"Alcohol. That's what we need right now."

I grabbed the bottle of Calvados by the neck, even though it was too early for me to start drinking. I tossed back the first glass at a gulp. I was in a hurry to get stunned.

After my third glass of Calvados I collapsed onto the sofa and pointed the remote control at the stereo. I pushed play and pumped the volume to maximum. The voice of Jimmy Wither-spoon exploded from the speakers, with the first lines of *Money's Gettin' Cheaper*.

Well, I can't afford to live,
I guess I'll have to try
Undertaker's got a union,
and it costs too much to die.

The night of the thirtieth day since the kidnapping, my cell phone rang and rang. I opened my eyes and the situation slowly swam into focus. I was stretched out on the sofa, the television was still on, and a soft-porn actress from the Seventies was singing the praises of the remarkable powers of an amulet that could be yours . . . I picked up the cell phone and looked at the caller ID. It was a number I had in my phone book. I sat bolt upright when I read the name.

"Sylvie!" I shouted with relief.

It was a woman's voice, but I'd never heard it before. Cold as a mountain stream. Strong German accent. Too strong to be real. "You still have to complete a task for which you have already been paid."

"Greta Gardner," I guessed.

"That's right. Then I don't need to go into detail."

"Tell me about Sylvie."

"There's an envelope in your mailbox downstairs," she announced, and hung up.

I galloped down the stairs. A medium-sized manila envelope, hand delivered. Inside was a photograph of a dancer in full regalia. The face was made up, there was a professional smile on her face, but the eyes that gazed into the lens when the picture was taken told a story of imprisonment, anger, and grief. I looked at the time and date, in red at bottom left. Sylvie was alive.

I galloped back up the stairs. I pounded on Max's door and phoned Beniamino. He answered on the second ring. It was just another sleepless night for him.

"Get over here," I panted. "Now."

The fat man came in. He looked at the picture. "I'm going to go make some coffee," he said, his voice quavering, and shut himself into the kitchen to weep in peace. I had too much alcohol and adrenalin in my system to do the same thing. I pulled open the drawer that had the photocopy of the passport of Greta Gardner in it. The retired detective De Angelis had described her as a nice piece of ass. If he was telling the truth, the photo didn't do her justice. She looked like a wan and harmless little blonde.

Until that moment I had been sure that the so-called Pierre Allain had just brought her along as camouflage. Instead, it turned out, she wore the pants in that couple. It was obvious the moment I heard her voice. It really is true: I don't understand a fucking thing about women.

Old Rossini kissed the photograph, then he wrapped his arms around both of us and stood silently, hugging us in his powerful grip. He ran his hand over his tear-streaked face. "My Sylvie."

Coffee. Then a solid hour of pounding his fist on the table, and a continuous refrain of: "Fuck, she's alive, fuck fuck fuck!"

And then: "We have to rescue her, yeah, we have to track down the bastards that stole the narcotics and then we need to make a deal. We're going to have to be careful though. Obviously that bitch has a plan in mind, she wants revenge . . ."

Once the emotional tempest of the news that Sylvie was alive had died down, we gradually managed to bring the situation into focus. Sylvie was being held prisoner by the accomplice—and perhaps the lover—of the late guy with the ring, and it was clear that the blonde with the German accent wasn't a bit happy about her boyfriend's premature death. She had certainly concocted some intricate and diabolical plan for a vendetta.

She'd arranged for Sylvie to be kidnapped, and then she'd let us stumble around in the dark for a month, maintaining complete radio silence. Then she gets in touch with a single specific request: find out who pulled the narcotics heist at the Institute of Legal Medicine. It had been more than two years. Why was it still so important? Whatever the story was, we had no choice. We had to take the assignment.

Even if she hadn't said so explicitly, clearly Sylvie's fate was bound up with that investigation. Of course, we weren't so naïve that we thought it would all culminate in a trade. In her plans, Rossini's woman would remain alive until we'd solved the case. Then Sylvie would be killed. Along with the three of us, I'd have to guess.

I picked up the photograph and looked at it again for what seemed like the thousandth time. She could have sent us any picture she wanted of Sylvie. Instead, she'd forced her to put on a costume and makeup and dance. That woman was clearly refined and twisted, and damned attentive to details.

"Greta Gardner has resources, money, and definitely an organization behind her," I said, thinking aloud. "When she realized that the guy with the ring was dead, she returned to base and calmly and coldly designed a plan to screw us."

"Yeah, we came to that conclusion an hour ago, Marco. That's what we've been talking about," replied Max with some concern.

"So the problem is that she has too big an advantage on us. If we play the game by her rules, we're bound to lose."

"Then what do you want to do?" asked Rossini.

"We have to play it our way."

"Which would be?"

"We have to split up," I replied. "I'll look for the guys who pulled the heist and you look for Sylvie. And Greta. Sylvie alive, and Greta dead. There's no other way out for us."

"Easier said than done," the fat man objected. "Our whole army is seated around this table."

"We have the photographs. We need to keep searching until we find somebody who's met them."

"Belgrade," Beniamino suggested.

"Excellent idea," I agreed. "You know plenty of people in the smuggling business. If they were informers at the time, then maybe there's a crooked cop out there who might remember them."

Max poured himself a cup of cold coffee, added sugar, and stirred for a long time, in a reverie. "It's a reasonable plan. But can you hold things down on your own?"

"I think so, though I doubt I'll find anything out. If you want to know the truth, I'm pretty sure that Greta doesn't give a shit about the heist. She just wants to watch us run for awhile, like gerbils on a treadmill."

The old smuggler turned and looked at Max. "I'm going home to pack and pick up some more money, and then I'll be back to pick you up."

Morena shook her head when she saw me. She said something to the tall elegant gentleman she was flirting with and came over to where I was standing.

"I hope you haven't gotten any funny ideas," she said under her breath. "That sex was strictly to celebrate the transaction."

"What if I'm ready to pay the 500 euros?"

She tossed her head toward the man she'd been talking with when I came in. "He'll pay that, but with fringe benefits. Plus, I like him better. At least I have something to talk about with him."

"I don't doubt it. Anyway, I'm here on business."

"The well known incident we've already discussed?"

"Right."

"Forget it. I'm not interested in reopening that can of worms."

"Just hear me out. You'll make twice as much money."

"He's going to take me to a resort in Tuscany for the weekend where you can't get in no matter how much money you have. He can get me in there. You can get me in trouble."

"Just put me in touch with your handsome policeman."

"I wouldn't dream of it."

She spun on her stiletto heels and marched back to her tall dark companion. I ordered a spritz and watched the little slut doing what she did. Actually, her new beau hardly looked like a dope. Quite the contrary. He knew exactly who he was dealing with. And he wasn't a loser who just couldn't find anything better for the weekend than a high-priced whore. "He's another guy who likes dangerous sluts," I thought, as I remembered Rossini's words.

But maybe, all things considered, it wasn't so true. Certainly, on the one hand, I was incapable of resisting the wiles of that kind of woman, even though I knew it would get me into trouble every time; on the other hand my ideal woman was very different: Virna.

But Virna had left me, and I hadn't lifted a finger to keep her from leaving. I popped a handful of salted peanuts into my mouth.

I was dying to see her again, but I was afraid that she'd reject me with one of those little sermons of hers in which every word is a knife to the heart. No, I wouldn't try to find her. I was too fragile in that period to take any further humiliations.

Morena and her date put on their overcoats and headed for the door. As he strode past me, he gave me a mocking little grin that I pretended not to notice.

The next day I woke up early so I could intercept De Angelis on his morning run. There was no one else I could think of, and the idea of a weekend of total inactivity while my friends were tracking down contacts in Belgrade struck me as intolerable.

I waited for the retired detective at his bar. He gave me a grim look. Those days, it seemed like nobody was happy to see me. I greeted him in a loud voice, including rank and full name.

He came toward me with both fists balled up and shoulders thrust forward. "Let me just make a quick phone call to a couple of friends who still have badges, and we'll see if you still feel like bothering me."

He hadn't lost his taste for threatening people, so I decided to remind him that not only is extorting money from foreigners staying in local hotels not considered friendly, it's not strictly legal.

He snickered. "I'm retired, and nobody gives a crap about that old story."

"Well, fair enough, but you have the money socked away somewhere, and I'm pretty sure I could find an investigating magistrate who doesn't owe you any debts of gratitude."

I must have pushed the right buttons. "What do you want?" he asked.

"I just want to talk about old times."

"I don't know shit about that narcotics heist."

"I'm happy to hear about rumors."

He pointed to the cashier. "Let me pay my check. I'll wait for you outside."

No one really seemed to understand why, back in 2004, that mountain of narcotics had accumulated in the basement store-rooms of the Department of Toxicology: bad management or an intentional tactic to facilitate a single big heist? The only thing that was clear was that someone with good information had taken advantage of the opportunity to haul it all away.

That much I already knew, however. What I didn't know was that in police circles the rumor was circulating that not even a single gram of the more than fifty kilos of narcotics had ever circulated in Italy. In the narcotics division, they were pretty sure that the drugs had been transported outside of the country long before anyone realized they were gone.

I told him about the two cops who paid a call on me at La Cuccia.

The former detective thought it sounded odd. He doubted they were officers from any of the normal departments. He thought it was an operation managed from the highest levels, using people from far away.

"Now get out of here. Let me enjoy my retirement in peace."

While I was driving back home, I got a call from Max. No news. They were buying drinks for half of Belgrade to get an in with the police.

Saturday evening at La Cuccia. A decent jazz quartet was playing, but I was ignoring it. A young woman asked me about Max.

She was cute but she sure wasn't friendly. It must have been the one that the fat man was going to invite for dinner the night before Sylvie was kidnapped. I made up a tale of woe about Max's aunt and how he had to go take care of her.

She wasn't buying it. She gave me a wry little grin.

"Has he heard the telephone was invented?"

"It's not much of a story, is it?" I admitted.

"It wasn't much when it was new; it's threadbare to say the least."

"There are no other women involved," I explained. "If I were you, I'd give him a second chance."

"Just tell him to stop wasting time. I'm overwhelmed by my suitors."

She couldn't manage to keep a straight face, and burst into laughter in a very attractive way.

"I'm Marco, pleased to meet you," I said, extending my hand.

"Teresa."

I bought her a drink and we talked until it was almost closing time.

On Sunday I got up and went out to buy my newspapers; I took a long stroll downtown. It was crowded with shoppers. Christmas wasn't far away now. I stopped off in Piazza Duomo for an aperitif.

I bought a paper cone of hot roasted chestnuts and then headed back home to go back to sleep.

The fat man woke me up in the middle of the afternoon. "We may have something," he said excitedly. "We'll be back tomorrow."

"Can you tell me anything more?"

"We have an invitation to dinner."

The following Wednesday we were all together, sitting around a table in a renowned restaurant in Mira, not far from Venice. There were six of us. Us three, a leading figure in Serbian organized crime, and his two bodyguards. The Serbian was named Pavle Stojkovic, and he was in charge of Northeast Italy for one of the few criminal organizations that had not been absorbed by the Belgrade mafia. Like many Eastern European gangsters, he had been an official in the state security apparatus until the Communist regime collapsed. Then he'd made the leap to the opposite side of the moat.

He was a cultivated gentleman, about fifty-five, affable and polite, conservatively dressed, and he had agreed to meet with us as a result of the intervention of a smuggler of considerable repute who had worked on many occasions with Beniamino. While waiting for the antipasto, he talked about classical music, letting us know he was a passionate opera fan. To intimate that he had gathered information about us, he wandered into the field of jazz and blues, and asked me to tell him about a number of musicians who had performed at La Cuccia.

"I attended a Maurizio Camardi concert in Belgrade," he said. "I went with my daughter."

He waited until he had scooped up his first forkful of risotto before he declared that he was ready to listen to our request. Max opened his leather briefcase and pulled out a file folder with the xeroxes of the passports of the supposed Pierre Allain and Greta Gardner, as well as photographs and information about Sylvie. Max handed the file to the bodyguard who sat next to Pavle Stojkovic, who in turn handed the papers to his boss. Gangsters like nothing so much as a healthy respect for hierarchies.

"The man is dead. We understand that he was an informant for the Serbian police," I explained. "The woman kidnapped Rossini's girlfriend. As ransom, she's demanding information on who was responsible for the theft of narcotics that took place at the Institute of Legal Medicine in Padua in 2004."

"What are you asking from the 'interests' I represent?"

"As much help as you can afford us."

He wanted to make sure that he had understood exactly what we were asking. "By which you mean?"

"Information. Anything you can give us to help ensure a positive outcome to this incident."

"To help us rescue my woman," Rossini spelled it out as clearly as he could.

"That's a big favor. You'd have to return the favor . . . with interest, as you Italians like to say."

"We are ready."

Stojkovic nodded. He looked Beniamino in the eye. "You have a very nice speedboat," he complimented him.

"The police don't have a single patrol boat that can outrun it."

"One crossing, with merchandise, for information about the theft," he proposed. "Two crossings for anything we can tell you about La Gardner or your lady within one week."

"Agreed. What kind of merchandise would I be transporting?"

"That's not a question I'm willing to answer. Any problem with that?"

The old smuggler shook his head, and the Serbian gangster smiled with satisfaction. "We aren't very well equipped for deep-sea transport. Perhaps in the future it might prove profitable for you to work with us."

Rossini stalled. "One thing at a time."

The bodyguard filled Pavle Stojkovic's glass with an excellent Friulian sauvignon. As the Serbian sipped it with evident approval, he began his story.

A substantial share of the heroin that had vanished so mysteriously from the Department of Toxicology belonged to the Kosovar mafia. Two-thirds of the heroin that was sold in Europe came from Afghanistan, was transported through Kosovo, where the opium was refined, and then forwarded on to the various European countries. Since 1997, the Kosovars had dominated the heroin market in Switzerland, Austria, Belgium, Germany, Hungary, Norway, the Czech Republic, and Sweden. In Italy, the Kosovars still had two rival groups: the Turks and the Serbians, but they struggled with considerable logistical disadvantages and a complete lack of "cooperation" from the intelligence services, which instead closed not one but both eyes when it came to the Kosovars.

"You mean that the heist was organized by the Italian intelligence services?"

"That's right."

"But why?"

"Kosovo is marching triumphantly toward a declaration of independence. But the KLA is not just an army of freedom fighters, it's also the armed branch of the Kosovar mafia, and its soldiers are the very structure of the criminal organization."

"That's the Serbian point of view," I objected, interrupting him.

He set his fork and knife down on his plate, interlaced the fingers of both hands, and rested his chin on them. "I am personally convinced that Kosovo belongs to my people, but we're talking business here: information in exchange for a specific service, and I am doing what I promised to do. I'm not engaging in an exchange of opinions in a bar, you understand that, don't you, Signore Buratti?"

"I understand perfectly, and I beg your pardon."

Another sip of wine, and he proceeded to explain the back-stage maneuverings that led up to the heist, while his grilled fish grew cold. The objective of the Kosovar mafia was to found a narcostate in the heart of Europe. For this to succeed, it was necessary that to the eyes of international public opinion the whole struggle should appear to be nothing more than a struggle for liberation from the rule of Belgrade waged by the Albanian majority. The Colombian mafia had already made agreements to use the territory as a point of arrival for its flow of cocaine; the Kosovars would arrange to distribute that cocaine through its own channels. And the United States would turn a blind eye in exchange for a number of substantial favors, including the construction of the largest and most expensive military base since the Vietnam War, Camp Bondsteel, subcontracted by the Pentagon to the usual beneficiary Halliburton, with the blessing of the former CEO, Dick Cheney. The camp is located strategically close to the trans-Balkan oil pipeline, which in the future is expected to bring oil from the Caspian Sea to the Adriatic, and it housed seven thousand men in more than three hundred buildings scattered over an area of a thousand acres.

Stojkovic continued to rattle off statistics and names, but he still hadn't told us anything significant or interesting about the heist. He came to the point after explaining the real estate interests at stake in the expulsion of the Serbian minority from Kosovo.

"One thing you should know is that the structure of the Kosovar mafia is very similar to that of the Calabrian 'ndrangheta. There isn't a commission at the top. The organization is structured horizontally, by biological families. That's why there are no turncoats or informers. You can't rat out your father and your brothers. But the families are often at war with one another. In 2004 the Padua prison was filling up with members of one of the three major clans that controlled the KLA. Among those convicts was Fatjon Bytyçi, the oldest son of a boss in Peć, who had been arrested with his girlfriend after a rival family informed on him to the police. To avoid a general gang war that would have created an international incident and undermined their larger objectives, the families called for a summit meeting to reach an agreement, and on that occasion the Italian intelligence services were asked to find a way of getting the Kosovars out of jail fast."

"Evidence Stolen, Acquittal in View?"—Max la Memoria sang out, reciting the headline that had appeared in a paper at the time.

"More or less. Some of them plea bargained for lighter sentences . . ."

"But not the son of the boss and his girlfriend, who were sent back to Kosovo."

"Exactly."

"And what happened to the narcotics stolen in Italy?"

He shrugged. "The intelligence services can always use that stuff."

Nothing more was said for the rest of the meal. Stojkovic skipped dessert, apologized for not having the time to drink a cup of coffee with us, and left the restaurant followed by his two goons.

"What the fuck is Greta Gardner going to do with this information?" the fat man said angrily. "I mean, it might have been useful immediately after the heist, but now?"

I revolved my coffee cup in its saucer absent-mindedly. "I told you before: she doesn't want the information; she just wants to make us do her bidding, like puppets on a string."

Then I turned to Beniamino. "You know they're going to fill your speedboat with heroin, right?"

"I'll do whatever it takes to bring Sylvie home."

There are cases where life gives you no options, where you're forced to betray your own principles. That's what had just happened to Old Rossini. I never expected to witness such a thing.

He touched my arm. "Are there problems, Marco?"

"Lots of problems, too many problems," I answered. "But whatever you do, I'll always be your friend."

Forty-eight hours later, one of Stojkovic's men showed up at Beniamino's house. The speedboat needed to depart in just one hour's time. The weather conditions weren't ideal for an open-sea voyage, but the merchandise had to arriva in Croatia the following morning, so that it could be forwarded on immediately.

While Rossini was battling the waves, Greta Gardner turned Sylvie's cell phone back on and called me.

"Have you completed the job?"

"Yes."

"Good, then you've taken care of your first debt."

"Then let Sylvie go."

"She's how you take care of your second debt," she told me. "There's no price on that one."

"Why should you kill her? Take it out on us."

"That's what I'm doing. You're going to have to live your lives in the knowledge that she will dance for many men, that she will satisfy the pleasures of many men, for years to come. Then she'll die."

"Can't we come to some sort of understanding?"

Greta Gardner laughed heartily. "In your letterbox you'll find another envelope. This is the last one."

"You don't want to know what we found out?"

"I already have all the answers. It was just a matter of principle."

She hung up, but this time I didn't rush downstairs. I walked down one step at a time. I felt as confused as a boxer nearing the end of his career. Greta's words had cut my legs out from under me. In the photograph this time, Sylvie was nude. So were the two men with her.

"Beniamino can never see this," I told Max a few minutes later.

"He has the right to know."

"In all likelihood, this is going to be the last picture we'll ever have of Sylvie. You want him to remember her like this?"

The fat man said nothing. I tore up the photograph.

"That was a fucked up thing to do, Marco," he scolded me. Then he added: "But I'm glad you did it."

"Alcohol?"

"No, thanks. I'm too depressed to drink."

"You think the Serbs will find anything?"

"I hope they will. It's in their own interest. They can use Beniamino and his speedboat."

Old Rossini called me mid-morning the next day to say that the bora wind out of the north was kicking up whitecaps as tall as houses, and that he would ride it out in a little bay in his speedboat, until the weather improved.

I was secretly pleased. I needed some time to recover. Beniamino knew me all too well. I didn't want to arouse his suspicions. He would have pushed to find out what had happened and sooner or later I'd tell him.

The cell phone rang again. This time it was Morena. I didn't want to talk to her; I didn't answer. I gave in the fourth time she called.

"What do you want?"

"I want to buy you a drink."

"You weren't very nice to me last time I saw you."

"You want an apology? Or would you rather I told you something that might interest you?"

"About that old case?"

"Right."

"I'm not interested in it anymore."

"I don't believe you."

"That's how it is, though. And besides, weren't you the one who said you didn't want to hear about it anymore?"

"I had a stroke of luck."

"Good for you, though I doubt you'll find any buyers."

She finally realized I meant it. I was about to hang up when she said: "Look, let's try it this way. I tell you what I found out, and if you're interested, you'll open your wallet."

"And I decide how much."

"I rely implicitly on your honesty and the goodness of your heart," she deadpanned.

Nice work, Morena. She'd roped me in for a second round. All my resolutions never to see her again had vanished into thin air the minute the phone rang.

It was raining, the traffic was even worse than usual, and finding a place to park in Padua had become an increasingly challenging proposition. I arrived late. The aperitif hour was over, the little café tables were already set for quick lunches. Frozen pasta dishes, heated up in a microwave, and fanciful "mega-salads." Morena was sitting with her back turned. Since she was a regular customer, she was allowed to go on nursing her spritz. I sat down across from her, and the first thing I noticed was the pair of oversized sunglasses. I delicately lifted them from the bridge of her nose. The bruise under her right eye was turning yellow, a sign that it was on the mend. I did some mental calculations.

"This was the guy who took you to that nonexistent resort in Tuscany, wasn't it?"

"One of his two friends. And the spa was a fucking mini-villa. I was the only one having no fun."

"Big disappointment, I'm sure."

"Pitfalls of the profession," she said, with a catch in her voice. "That's what my handsome policeman told me."

"And he's not going to lift a finger to help you."

"Wouldn't dream of it."

I sighed. "You want me to tell you what I think?"

"I know, I know: the years pass, and the older I get the more men are going to take advantage of me."

I thought of Sylvie and what she was going through: I suddenly lost my desire to teach anyone a lesson.

I ordered a couple of sandwiches and a glass of red and thought: At least Morena is free to choose.

"I always wanted to be in business for myself, but I think the time may have come to sign up with one of these luxury escort services." She sighed: "I missed my chance when I couldn't manage to marry 'the right guy.' By now, I'd be coddled, well cared for, and revered."

I changed the subject. "So, what's the news?"

"It was a gang of policemen who stole the narcotics."

"Crap."

"No, it's the truth. They work in Friuli and they had an accomplice on the inside. My handsome policeman is one of a team that's tapping their phones."

"And he told you this?"

"Yes."

So you'd come tell me, I thought to myself. But if he was trying to get me off the case, why would he invent a story that involved crooked cops?

"They kept the stuff hidden until six months ago, and now they're handing over a kilo a week to a gang they have dealing it for them."

"My wallet stays in my pocket. I'm not interested."

"Fuck you," she grumbled disappointedly.

"Give me the name of that guy and his cell phone number."

"What, have you become the avenger of mistreated hookers?"

"Yes, but I'm not doing it for you," I thought. This is for Sylvie. I couldn't get that damned photograph out of my head. "You going to give them to me or not?"

She slipped her hand into her purse and pulled out a business card. "I don't need it anymore."

Rocco Ponzano was barely 5' 7" but he was a born hitter. When he was fourteen, to keep him away from bad company in the alleys of Genoa, his father locked him up in a boxing gym.

He came out four years later, but the same friends were waiting for him; they'd been wondering what had become of him, and they showed him the way to prison, where I met him. Now he was free and he lived in Padua. He worked for a cooperative that provided counseling and aid to ex-convicts.

He'd gone straight, but he couldn't refuse to do this favor for me. He owed me.

The shitbag who'd gotten his jollies by punching Morena in the eye lived in a villa in the center of Este, a lovely town in the Venetian provinces, with his wife and daughter. That same evening, when he got out of his 50,000 euro automobile and turned to go into his house, he found himself looking at Rocco. Rocco didn't say a word; he just fired off a series of violent and very accurate punches, focusing on the nose and eyebrows.

A few hours later, when I was sure that he'd been released from the emergency room, I called him from a public phone booth. I gave him a little lecture on the idea behind good manners. He swore to me on his daughter's head that he understood the lesson.

Then I lost control. "What the fuck is the matter with you all?" I screamed into the phone. "Don't you know how to have normal sex anymore? Do you always have to be violent fucking bullies?"

I smoked a couple of cigarettes in my car with the windows rolled up, and then I drove to La Cuccia, where I found Max; he had spent the whole day in his apartment. He showed me the photograph of Fatjon Bytyçi that was taken the day he was arrested.

"He looks more like a dirt farmer than the heir to a mafia empire. Look at how the fuck he's dressed."

He wasn't wrong. "These Kosovars are still a little rustic. They'll find their style when Hollywood discovers them."

"You watch too much television."

"You can never watch enough. What else have you found on him?"

"Nothing."

"I saw Morena." I told him what she'd said about the gang of policemen.

He waved one hand in the air with a gesture of annoyance. "Bullshit. Even if it was true, it wouldn't help us find Sylvie."

Pavle Stojkovic kept his word; on the seventh day he summoned us to a meeting. This time, it was in an elegant pastry shop in Vicenza. He asked Rossini how the trip had gone, and said he was sorry that it had been so long and challenging. He seemed to mean what he said.

We were surrounded by old people and mothers telling their children not to get chocolate and whipped cream on their clothing. Everything kept getting more Christmas-y. All around us was glitter and sparkle and blinking lights, making those days seem even more unreal and tragic.

The Serbian gangster ordered a cup of tea and waited to be served without saying a word. He finally began speaking, and just in time: a few seconds longer and Rossini might have lost it and slammed him against the wall.

"We haven't found out anything about Greta Gardner," he explained. "But we have learned that a belly dancer, who matches the description of your kidnapped girlfriend, has recently begun performing in a bordello on the outskirts of Grenoble."

I glanced over at Beniamino's face. He seemed to be carved out of marble. Stojkovic looked him right in the eye.

"I'm sorry to have to tell you this . . . It's a very particular sort of place."

My friend gulped. "A gang bang parlor?"

"I'm afraid so."

For an instant I could barely breathe. Gang rapes. The men would watch her dance and then, once they were thoroughly excited, take off their pants.

"The address," Rossini snarled. "Tell me where she is. I'm going to get her back."

"There's a problem; I assure you, I had no say in this decision."

"What's the problem?"

"I can only give it to you after you do two more trips."

The smuggler's mouth snapped open in amazement. He was too appalled to react.

"How can you be so pitiless?" I demanded indignantly.

"This is just business to us, Signore Buratti."

Max la Memoria broke in. "The agreement was information first, merchandise transported afterwards."

"In Belgrade they're worried that if something should happen to Signore Rossini, then the merchandise would not be transported. The value of the merchandise is much greater than that of the woman. I feel sure you can understand our point of view."

Finally Beniamino found the strength to speak. "In the smuggling business, everyone knows me, they know that I've always kept my word. You can't treat me like this."

"Yes, we can," the Serbian cut him off.

"How long do you think she can hold out?"

"That's not my problem."

"If she winds up dying, it will certainly become your problem."

"I appreciate your feelings, but threatening me isn't a very good idea."

One of his goons had slipped his right hand into the left sleeve of his heavy jacket. The first one of us who moved would get a knife wound for his trouble. The other one had his hand in the pocket of his overcoat, certainly gripping a pistol.

But Rossini was a desperate man, betrayed and worn out by tension and exhaustion. In a word, dangerous. I felt sure of it when I saw that he was carefully noting the location of the two thugs. He was calculating his odds of managing to hit Stojkovic before they could intervene.

I dug my fingernails into his thigh and shook him. "The kids," I hissed. "The children."

"What?" He looked around realized he was in a pastry shop full of innocent people.

He drained his glass of beer at a gulp and gave me a grateful glance.

Now it was my chance to negotiate. "Seven days from today for both trips."

"I can't guarantee it."

"Help us," I implored. "You're in charge here."

He stood up. "I'll see what I can do."

He walked out of the shop accompanied by one of his body-guards. The other one stayed behind with us, sitting and staring at Beniamino. He was going to stand up and leave only once his boss was safe.

A few minutes later, the cell phone rang. Unknown caller. I answered anyway. It was Stojkovic. "Okay, we have a deal in seven days if your friend can leave on his holidays tomorrow morning."

We walked for a while along the porticoes, in silence, catching our breath.

"You go to Yugoslavia, and Max and I will go to Grenoble to lay the groundwork. We're going to need a safe house, and we need to check out the escape routes."

Rossini shook his head. "Greta Gardner would know you were there, and that would spell death for Sylvie."

"We'd be careful."

"Beniamino is right," the fat man broke in. "If she can deliver two envelopes to our door, it means she has someone working for her in the area. There'd be nothing easier than for her to keep us under surveillance."

I glared at him, but the cat was out of the bag.

"Why did you say two envelopes?" Rossini asked.

"Ask Marco."

"The second envelope had a picture I chose not to show you. I tore it up."

"How many?"

"Two."

He nodded and turned his face toward a shop window, where he pretended to be looking at sets of porcelain. "I'll ask Luc and Christine to go to Grenoble."

"Who the fuck are they?" I'd never heard their names.

Luc Autran and Christine Duriez. Husband and wife, and partners on the job. Their specialty was armed robberies. They lived in Marseilles, but they were careful not to pull any of their capers near home. They worked the French provinces and often worked outside the country. Belgium, Spain, and one job in Italy. An armored car in the Turin area. Rossini had come up with the plan.

Their two accomplices, a pair of Portuguese, had been arrested a few months later trying to make off with the take from a robbery at a small bank in Germany. Excellent in terms of execution but no good in terms of planning.

"What about the duo from Marseilles: are they good at planning?"

"They've never been caught. They know what they're doing."

"I thought you met this Luc in jail."

"No, I met his uncle there."

I looked down on the Isère river from the cable car. The dark water flowed sluggishly. My back was to the mountain. In front of me, beyond the riverbank was the old Italian quarter, with signs for restaurants and pizzerias, with names that harked back to places that emigrants had left with cardboard suitcases and empty stomachs.

Max was sitting across from me, his eyes gazing at the mountain peak. Beniamino was talking quietly with Luc and Christine. The rescue team, in its entirety. Sitting in a circle, we filled up one of the little cable cars, a steel and plexiglas bubble that carried tourists from the city up to the Fort de la Bastille. Up there, you could enjoy a spectacular view of the entire valley.

We had arrived the night before from Italy, after taking great care to make sure no one was following us. Our final destination was Chambéry, about twenty miles away from Grenoble. There the duo from Marseilles had rented an apartment in an old building downtown for a month. The landlady was the widow of an armed robber. She led an apparently respectable life working as a server in a bakery, but she wasn't above rounding out her salary by renting her place to old friends of her late husband. Two bedrooms, a bathroom, and a kitchen.

Luc had awakened us at eight on the dot with coffee and croissants. I opened my eyes and found myself face-to-face with a skinny guy with a handlebar mustache, decidedly out of fashion, but I felt sure that his look was a professional tool and that just before he pulled a job he always shaved that mustache.

His face was creased with deep wrinkles even though he wasn't much older than forty. Leather jacket, jeans, work boots. He could easily have been mistaken for a factory worker or a carpenter.

I shook hands with him but, since I didn't know a word of French, I left it up to Max and Beniamino to keep the conversation going. A short while later, Christine appeared. She was wearing an extra-large cotton t-shirt that she had used as pajamas. She was about thirty-five, hair cropped short, a face with strong but pleasing features. She couldn't have been any taller than 5' 5", skinny, and small-breasted, but clearly an habituée of some good gym. Dark, resolute eyes.

When she saw Rossini she threw her arms around him and kissed his bald forehead joyfully. Then she said something about Sylvie and the room fell into silence. She pulled out two unfiltered cigarettes, clamped them both between her lips and lit them, and then handed one to Beniamino. It was a gesture that indicated friendship and respect, not just a business relationship. If my friend had turned to them, it meant they were professionals who knew how to do their jobs, but it also meant that they had heart and a modicum of decency.

We had followed their car to Grenoble along a heavily traveled provincial highway. The Alps surrounding the city were lightly dusted with snow. Another year of high temperatures. If tourists wanted to ski for the Christmas holidays, they would have to settle for artificial snow this year.

That morning the sun still hadn't emerged from behind the clouds and on the summit of Mont Rachais, where the fort had been built, a bone-chilling wind was blowing. We slipped into a café for a hot drink. Pretending to be tourists, we toured the museum and wandered around looking at the other structures. Only at the end did we climb onto the roof of the central fortification, known as the Belvédère Vauban. From here we had an excellent panoramic view. Luc handed us a powerful pair of binoculars and spoke for a few minutes about the mountains that towered on our right, telling stories about incidents from the French Resistance for the benefit of any nosy visitors. Then he turned to the city. Every so often Max would whisper a few words of translation in my ear.

Finally we moved over to the left side. Another fort, another mountain peak. They both had the same name: Saint-Eynard. On the slope of the mountain we could see the little town of Corenc, just under four thousand inhabitants scattered over different neighborhoods. A discreet village filled with handsome villas. In one of these villas, Sylvie was being held captive. Through the lenses of the binoculars, I could make out a large pre-war house, but we were too far away to make out any details.

"I can't take you down to see it up close in daylight," Christine explained. "I walked by the place at three different times of day, and there was always someone on the lookout at a window. I noticed they were checking out passing cars, too."

"I got pretty close late at night," Luc said. "The dogs guarding the other villas caught my scent and started barking, but nobody left the comfort of their beds to look out the window. In the villa's front courtyard two large luxury automobiles were parked, the windows were shuttered. That's all I saw."

"For a whorehouse, there's not a lot of visitors," the woman commented.

"Well, it's not exactly a whorehouse," Max la Memoria started to explain, but his voice wavered out when realized that if he went on he'd only be adding to Rossini's pain. But Old Rossini proved once again that he was a man of profound courage.

"There's nobody but Sylvie in there," he said softly. "And the only way that men can come in is if there are at least three of them. Three at a time, if you see what I mean."

Christine gripped his arm and chewed out a long and elaborate curse.

"So basically we don't know shit," the smuggler went on. "And we have to rely on what that bastard Pavle Stojkovic told us."

The Serbian gangster, once Beniamino had completed his two crossings, had finally revealed where Sylvie was being held prisoner; he had added that, according to their informant, the "house" would shut down for Christmas, and the belly dancer would be moved to another location.

"I'm going in as soon as it's dark and I'm getting her out of there," Old Rossini announced.

No one had any objections. Luc pointed to a road running around the outskirts of the city; it skirted a cemetery and then ran over a nearby bridge. "That's how we get out of here. That's how we come in and that's how we leave."

"You guys don't have to come. You've already done too much."

"No, if we come then we have you on the hook: you'll have to organize another fat job in Italy to repay us," Christine joked.

"And obviously Max and I are coming with you," I said.

"You've never even held a gun in your life."

"We could help without being armed."

"We could drive, for example," the fat man suggested.

"Maybe we could use them as a diversion," Luc proposed. "They ring the doorbell and say they're from a religious cult of some kind. We'll be waiting in the garden, hidden right next to the front door."

Rossini shook his head, skeptically. "That'd be far too unusual; it'd put them on alert. The only thing we can do is to jimmy open a door or window, get inside, and see what happens next."

"It's not much of a plan," Christine pointed out.

"We have a few hours to improve on it. More important, how can we keep from making noise?"

"Three .22 caliber carbine rifles, with silencers and ten-shot clips. Brand new, in the original packaging, stolen just a couple of days ago from a gun shop in Vienne," Luc answered. "Here in France they're legal. They're used for nighttime hunting. But if everything goes bad fast, we have three heavy sawed off shotguns."

"What about the vehicles?"

"Two cars. They aren't anything special, but we switched license plates with plates taken from identical models. They should do."

At six o'clock that evening Beniamino, Luc, and Christine, armed and wearing camouflage, climbed silently over the wall into the garden from the back of the house. The dogs in the neighboring villas began barking as soon as they approached the house. Max and I, at the wheels of the two getaway cars, kept an eye on the windows of the houses along the street. No movement. The residents must have been accustomed to false alarms. It was probably enough for a dog or any other kind of animal to walk past to trigger a chorus of howls. It was hardly a crime-ridden neighborhood. In fact, it was a perfect neighborhood for someone to lay low if they were wanted by the law. Or a perfect neighborhood to hide a kidnap victim.

At 6:15 we parked in front of the villa. I got out first and peered through the gaps in the wrought-iron fence, the one across the driveway.

"I only see a Mercedes."

"They've been in there for a long time."

A couple of minutes later the little pedestrian gate leading to the walk swung open. For a brief instant Christine appeared, dressed in dark clothing and with a ski mask over her face. She gestured to us to enter through the gate.

"Sylvie is locked in a room on the second floor. The door is armor-plated, and we can't find the key. You go on in; I'll keep a lookout down here."

Max translated for me as we slipped our ski masks over our heads.

The furnishings were expensive, modern, recently purchased, and in the crassest of taste. We stepped over a dead man in the middle of the hallway that led to the stairs, and I understood there was nobody left to question.

We reached Beniamino and Luc as they were struggling to pry the door frame away from the wall. We could clearly hear Sylvie's muffled cries as she called out her bandit lover's name over and over.

"Find the fucking key," the smuggler shouted, pointing to a door.

We walked into a study of sorts; inside were two more men, shot dead. The first guy was stretched out face-down on a thick white carpet, with a puddle of blood slowly spreading from under his corpse. The other dead guy was slouched in an office chair, behind an impressive desk. There were three or four bulletholes in his chest.

I pointed to him and told my partner: "I know this guy."

"That's Fatjon Bytyçi. This villa belongs to the Kosovar mafia."

I stepped closer to the corpse of the son of the godfather of Peć and started emptying his pockets. Nothing useful. I noticed that he had a heavy gold chain around his neck that I hadn't seen in the photograph in the newspaper. I slipped the chain off his neck and found a key at the end of it. Short, flat, shaped like a butterfly.

"Got it!" I exclaimed and ran out of the room.

Rossini grabbed it out of my hand and fitted it into the lock. The door swung open and before our eyes emerged a ghost of the woman we'd known.

He made a move to seize her in a crushing embrace but he stopped, bewildered, suddenly fearful that he'd shatter that profoundly fragile figure. She realized why he'd stopped and, covering her face, burst into tears.

Beniamino set his rifle down. "My love," he murmured as he gently gathered her in his arms.

"We need to get out of here," Luc blurted out.

He was right. I looked around. The fat man wasn't there. He was still in the study, rummaging through the desk drawers.

"Forget about that. We have to get out of here."

"Why was Sylvie being held prisoner by Fatjon Bytyçi? Doesn't that strike you as an unlikely coincidence?"

"Maybe so. I'll give that a little thought sometime when I'm not in danger of spending the rest of my life in a French prison."

Two cars, two teams. I was driving the one with Beniamino and Sylvie—barefoot and wrapped in a blanket. The married couple from Marseilles were with Max.

"I'm happy to see you again," I told her. "You have no idea."

She reached out a hand and touched my hair. Beniamino whispered to his love constantly until we got back to our parked cars. Christine slipped into our car to give Sylvie a kiss, then she joined her husband in their car. They would take care of disposing of the rifles by tossing them into the icy waters of the Isère, then staight home.

Sylvie was in no condition to drive all the way back to Punta Sabbioni. She needed time to recover. They'd stay as long as necessary in the house in Chambéry. Rossini gathered her into his arms and carried her into the apartment as if she were a little girl. He laid her gently on the bed in the bigger of the two bedrooms.

Max and I came in to say hello and goodbye to her, but she turned her back to us, her face to the wall. It was understandable.

"Tell her that we love her."

"When the time is right," Beniamino answered, a bit distractedly. He was at once happy and broken. He hadn't expected to find her so ravaged. Neither had we. But in retrospect, it was predictable enough.

"There's something you need to know," the fat man started to tell him. "The dead man in the study, the one in the office chair, is Fatjon Bytyçi."

"So?"

"It was to get him and the men of his clan out of prison that they arranged the narcotics heist from the Institute of Legal Medicine."

"OK, and that means what to me?"

"It means that none of this adds up. We have to figure out what kind of spider's web we've wandered into . . ."

Old Rossini seized him by the arms. "Listen. Right now I care about Sylvie, nothing else. I don't give a crap who died in that office."

"Well, the Kosovar mafia may feel differently."

Tears filled his eyes. "In that room is the woman I love. She needs me right now. And you're coming at me with this bull-shit?"

Max turned a bewildered gaze in my direction.

"You're right. Get in touch as soon as you can," I said, as I hustled my partner toward the door.

I'm running out of money," Rossini sighed.

"That's a problem," Max commented. "How's Sylvie?"

The old bandit took a long pause while he tried to find the right words. "She hasn't danced again. That's not all. She doesn't move, she doesn't live the way she once did. She's lost her spirit."

His lips were curled in a bitter sneer, his eyes no longer laughed the way they once had: the most unmistakable signs of defeat. And defeat wasn't something that Old Rossini was used to.

He hadn't found a way to bring Sylvie back, to heal her, but he'd never give up. He would stay by her side even if meant enduring a living hell. It was his way of loving. Bandit love.

I turned to look out the window at the lake. Since I'd come to live in this apartment in Lugano it'd become second nature to me. It helped me think.

Beniamino had just arrived a few hours earlier from Beirut, where he and Sylvie had taken shelter under the protection of a powerful Druse family. He'd smuggled contraband liquor and cigarettes with the Druses during the civil war in Lebanon.

It had been two years and six days since we rescued Sylvie. We'd been obliged to vanish from our old haunts. The old smuggler had sold the villa and the speedboat, Max and I had found a buyer for the entire farmhouse, with the upstairs apartments and La Cuccia: we needed cash to flee the revenge of the Kosovars, Greta Gardner, and anyone else who might be interested in getting us out of the way. Twenty-four months after the raid on the villa in Corenc, we still hadn't managed to figure out with any certainty exactly what had happened in that intricate story.

Given the presence of the corpse of Fatjon Bytyçi, we understood that if we waited around we'd be killed one by one. We fled. The only way to dodge the bullets of those organized criminals was to split up and cut all ties with our old lives. It would have been much more complicated to escape the police, in the age of high-tech security.

Max la Memoria hadn't wandered all that far from Padua. He'd taken shelter in Fratta Polesine, a small town filled with old villas and socialist and radical traditions. He'd continued to update his files and had established a friendship with a young architect, his family, and his friends. Together, they'd decided to try to refine a wine known as the Incrocio Cagnoni. They were chasing their dream of distilling the first brandy in the area.

I'd crossed the Swiss border and stopped at Lugano. I had a hunch that it was the right place to wait for events to evolve. There, time moves at a different pace.

And it turned out I'd been right. "Where nothing ever happens," I wrote in an email to Max, "the weeks and months flow over you without leaving a mark. If fate or distraction decided that I would spend the rest of my days here, I don't think I could bring myself to regret it."

I wasn't bored, either. Long walks, bars, concerts, theaters, movies, lots of newspapers, and the occasional book. I lived like a ghost, or like a tourist who'd enjoyed himself so much that he'd never gone back to his everyday life. Even if there had never been anything everyday about my life; at the most, an appearance of the everyday tied up with the fact that I helped to run La Cuccia, but only when I wasn't on a case.

I'd never been a "regular" citizen, and I'd never wanted to become one. When I was young and I sang blues in clubs, it didn't take me long to figure out that my whiteboy voice wasn't going to be good enough to build a genuine career. So I'd have to figure out something if I wanted to get old without too much suffering.

But prison had tossed my plans in the air. When I got out, an obsession with the truth turned me into an unlicensed private investigator. I'd earned a reputation among the lawyers who hired me as something of a crusader; but I was just doing my best to survive the cruel trick fate had played on me without having to pretend I was moving on and forgetting the past.

Still, even that way of life eventually turned into a routine. I'd found an equilibrium of sorts, and I could have gone on that way for many years to come, and finally retired. I'd even started laying the groundwork by putting aside some savings. But the death of the Kosovar Mafioso had ruined all that.

At that point, Lugano had wrapped me in its motionless, sleepy, well scrubbed beauty, making the loss of places and things of the past a little easier to take.

Actually, that's not exactly how it had gone. Virna had played her part: she was my one violation of the basic rules of security. I had felt the urgent need to leave my collection of blues records and CDs in trusted hands. And so I found myself ringing the doorbell of her new house. At first she told me I was an idiot for getting into the kind of trouble that forced me to flee the country. Then she agreed to take care of that important piece of my life. Finally, she slipped a piece of paper with her email address into the pocket of my leather jacket.

Many months later, perched on a bar stool in a five-star hotel, I noticed a woman using a public internet terminal. She was smiling as she typed an email. I hurried home and wrote to Virna from the same address I was using to stay in touch with Max and Beniamino.

She wrote back and said that she'd come to visit me, but that I'd have to trust her and tell her where I was hiding. A couple of weeks later I went to pick her up at the train station. She'd changed. She was even prettier with a big belly.

"Jesus, you're pregnant!"

"Well, as far as that goes, I'm also married."

"Who's the lucky guy?"

"A good man who I want to raise a child with."

"I still haven't heard the world 'love'."

"You haven't hugged me yet and you're already busting my chops?"

"Sorry," I muttered as I gathered my courage to embrace her. "I'm just a little surprised."

"I'm tired. Take me home."

She undressed and lay down on the bed to rest. I walked over and delicately placed my ear against her belly.

Virna ran her fingers through my hair. "Sleeping."

"How far along are you?"

"Fifth month."

"Boy or girl?"

"Girl."

"Happy?"

"Happy."

"Was it an accident or did you try to have a baby?"

"Time was running out, and getting pregnant at my age is no walk in the park."

"And you wear yourself out coming to visit old lovers?"

"I just felt like seeing you," she murmured, snuggling into my arms.

We lay that way, in silence. It was nice, if somewhat disturbing. I knew that she didn't have the slightest intention of coming back into my life, but she hadn't shut me out of hers completely. In fact, she'd decided to try to find a little corner of her life just for the two of us. I'd settle for it; it was more than I expected.

After a while she got up and went into the bathroom, and when she came out she was completely nude. I knew that way she had of breathing and nibbling at her lips; I took off my pants. Virna lay down in the middle of the bed, grabbed me by the shoulders, pushed me toward her belly. "You remember how I like it?"

After the birth of her baby, she brought her back to meet me. "I'd like you to meet Emma."

"Ciao, Emma," I muttered uneasily. The open innocence of little children always made me uncomfortable. No one was innocent in my world.

Virna laughed heartily. "You should see yourself . . ."

Later, I watched her nurse Emma. When they left, their scent stayed around for another couple of days to keep me company.

They came back to see me once a month.

"What do you tell your husband?" I asked her during one of her visits.

"Certainly not the truth," she replied brusquely. "He wouldn't understand and I don't want to lose him. I love him. I love you too, Marco, but in a different way. You're the men of my life."

"Can I say that I love you?"

"Certainly not. You need to keep that to yourself. You'd ruin everything."

Right. I never have understood a fucking thing about women.

On the other hand, I hadn't seen my friends till that very day. It was difficult. We were all in the grip of strong emotions, but we kept ourselves pretty buttoned up at first. We had some important decisions to make. After that, we could drink to our friendship. The alcohol would bring words to the surface that had been tamped down far too long; the time would come to exchange confidences. I couldn't wait to tell them about Virna.

"I haven't spent much of my money," the fat man told Rossini. "If you need some . . ."

"I've got some savings," I tossed in.

"Thanks. I've decided to put together a gang. I've got a tip on a knockover that'll take care of us for a long, long time," Rossini announced.

"What do you mean 'us'? We're not armed robbers. We never have been."

"Well, this time you'll make a stretch, unarmed, of course," Beniamino shot back. "There's so much money in play here that we could really take care of all our debts once and for all. Nowadays everything's so damned expensive."

I exchanged glances with Max. After 737 days of devoting all his energy and time to Sylvie, Old Rossini had made up his mind to wage war against the bastards who had made us dance like marionettes and then forced us into hiding. He hadn't exaggerated his determination, he'd spoken prudently and cautiously, but he had clearly referred to a vendetta as the sole possible form of justice.

To talk about returning our lives to normal was excessive, especially considering that we'd murdered the heir to a mafia family. There was no getting around their code of honor.

"Is it worth it?" I wondered aloud. "Does it make sense to risk losing more than we already have?"

Rossini shrugged. "You may have a point, but Sylvie has been screaming in her sleep for two years now, and I can't even touch her with the tip of my little finger. I can't imagine living like this without making sure that everyone that had anything to do with her kidnapping pays for what they did."

"Beirut isn't just a hop, skip, and a jump," I objected. "What are you going to do with Sylvie?"

"I have her blessing. She wants me to kill off her nightmares."

It all made perfect sense. I turned to the fat man. "What about you?"

"We're friends, aren't we? That alone is reason enough, but no matter what, it makes sense to take this thing to its logical conclusion, because sooner or later they'll fuck us anyway."

"What do you mean?"

"On February 17 of this year, Kosovo unilaterally pro-claimed independence. It's a farce packaged with ribbons and a bow for world public opinion. In fact, now the mafia can enjoy greater freedom, and greater protection, and in the past few months it has established itself more securely in Northeast Italy. In other words, before it's all over, they'll have accumulated the resources and the contacts to track us down."

I lit a cigarette and handed the pack to Beniamino. "Max hasn't been wasting his time."

"I felt sure of it. The only one who's been twiddling his thumbs is you."

"Let me guess," I said. "After the robbery of the century we're all going to work together to track down the mysterious Greta Gardner?"

Old Rossini shifted uneasily in his chair. "Before being sold to that animal Fatjon Bytyçi, it was Sylvie's misfortune to meet La Gardner in the flesh. She refused to tell me the details, but the meeting wasn't pleasant."

I gave up. "Look, I'm baffled here. Why would a woman with ties to the Serbian intelligence services sell a woman to a Kosovar Mafioso?"

"We'll have to ask Pavle Stojkovic about that, someday," replied the fat man, extracting a laptop computer from a bag. "Pavle Stojkovic and Greta are certainly in cahoots, but the Kosovars have no idea that they are responsible for the murder of Fatjon Bytyçi."

"How can you be sure of that?"

"Because now the boundary with eastern Europe is con-trolled by a cartel. Aside from the Croatians, the Bulgarians, the Hungarians, the Romanians, the Turks, and the Russians, now they're part of it too, just part of a big happy family of interna-tional mafias."

"So they finally found grounds for an agreement," Rossini commented.

Max explained that they had been forced into it. On the one hand because the superhighway between the eastern border and Padua carries on a daily basis most of the illegal merchandise entering and leaving Italy. That made it indispensable to control the traffic to avoid losing shipments or having to hand out too many bribes. On the other hand, shortly thereafter the Italian government would pass a law making it a crime to be an illegal, undocumented immigrant: anyone who wanted to try to make money in Italy would be obliged to turn to the various structures organized by the various mafias. And in this sector the Kosovars were way ahead of everyone else. They had already set up travel agencies that, for the moderate fee of 3,500 euros, provided fake German tourist visas that were valid for the entire Schengen Area. For another 8,000 euros, they could put together fake marriages and, if you could afford it, they could purchase the complicity of a cooperative official.

"And we're going to let the Kosovars know that Stojkovic is not a trustworthy partner?"

"We'll take that possibility into consideration when the time is right," the fat man replied. "First we have to figure out what they know about us."

"I don't think that we can just go and ask them what they know."

Max smiled. "We won't need to."

Rossini went into the kitchen to make some coffee. He came back with a tray in his hand and another question in mind. "Why did they clean up the crime scene in Corenc, and bring the corpses back to Peć just in time for the funerals?"

"Evidently they couldn't ruin the territory for themselves by revealing their presence."

"Or else they were ashamed to let the corpse of the godfather's son be found in a gang bang parlor," the fat man objected. "From what I've been able to find out, Fatjon was a fucking sadist with women. In Mitrovica, during the massacre of the ethnic Serbian minority, he was involved in a lot of war crimes. This might be the reason he was sent out of the country. After all, he didn't count much in the family politics."

I stepped out to buy something for dinner in a *rosticceria* that specialized in delicacies from southern Italy, where I usually did my shopping for pasta and fresh cheeses.

"Well, we have some guests with a healthy appetite today," the shopowner observed. If she'd had any idea of the topics of conversation during our meal, she would have certainly learned to keep her nose out of other people's business.

After the antipasto we decided to discuss the first part of our plan: the robbery that would provide us with the money we'd need to take on our enemies, or to flee even further away if things turned ugly.

"As I was saying," Beniamino began, "I've decided to start a gang. I've contacted Luc and Christine and two Germans I met in Beirut."

"Target?"

"A goldsmith's workshop in the province of Alessandria, north of Genoa. The safe is a piggy bank for a gang of Lebanese Maronite drug dealers. They'll only report the gold that they're legally holding. If it all goes smoothly, our cut should be about three million euros."

"That fucking safe will be tough to get into . . ."

"But we have a mole, an inside man. The managing director of the company."

I drained off my glass of red wine. "We're not going to find a gang of wise guys on our tail after we pull off the job, are we? If the Maronites suspect he's involved, they'll put the screws to him and he'll talk."

Old Rossini grinned. "But they'll never know about us. They don't even know we exist."

"This job comes straight from the Druses?"

"That's right."

Max suggested an added detail. "It might be nice to put out word that the mastermind behind the robbery is Pavle Stojkovic."

"When do you plan to pull off the job?"

"January 19th. That's a Monday."

I looked at my friends in horror, "That's less than twenty days, and we don't have the slightest idea of what we'll do afterwards."

"I'm leaving for Beirut in three days. Sylvie is waiting for me; we're going to celebrate New Year's together. We'll have plenty of time to develop a solid plan."

The fat man didn't blink. He rolled a slice of prosciutto around a sun-dried tomato packed in oil. He slowly chewed and then shook his head. "There's nothing you can do about it: Italian cooking doesn't work when you try to blend weird tastes and flavors."

Then he leveled his index finger at me. "I'm doing the cooking on the night of the 31st."

"I figured you were heading back to Fratta Polesine."

"I wish. They know how to celebrate there. But I think we have some planning to do."

Walking through my home town like an illegal immigrant. It was an odd feeling. From time to time I'd cross paths with people I'd known all my life. They wouldn't give me a second glance. For that matter, though, it was practically impossible to recognize me. I'd cut my hair short and grown a stylish little goatee, I was wearing a pair of fake eyeglasses, and I had radically changed my style of dress.

In Verona I'd walked into a pretty expensive boutique. While talking with the sales clerk, I pointed to a fifty-year-old gentleman with a wealthy appearance and said: "I want to dress like him."

The sales clerk was about sixty; he'd been doing this work for more than forty years. He looked me up and down carefully and said: "Too late. You'll never pull it off. But if we lower our sights a little and restrict our ambitions, we might achieve something vaguely similar and just barely acceptable."

He was right. I felt uncomfortable in a jacket and tie, and it wasn't just a matter of habit.

As I was leaving the store, he asked me to recite the combinations of colors and fabrics, and I got every one of them wrong. He shook his head resignedly and wished me good luck.

I'd never spent that much money on clothing in my life, but I could easily have afforded to buy everything in the shop. The robbery had brought us vast wealth: 511 kilograms of gold: well over 16,000 troy ounces. Luckily, since there had been seven of us, we managed to clean out the entire vault full of gold. The job was as quick and easy as the narcotics heist at the Institute of Legal Medicine. We had the security codes so we were able to deactivate the alarms, sneak into the workshop in the middle of the night, and conceal ourselves in the bathrooms. There we waited for the morning arrival of the employees and the owner with the keys to the vault, which could only be unlocked at 9 am.

"Don't do this to me," he'd implored us, collapsing to his knees.

Beniamino, Luc, Christine, and the two Germans had worked swiftly and methodically like the professionals that they were; they even remembered to utter a few words in Serbian from time to time, for the benefit of the wide-eyed, presumably wide-eared robbery victims. Max and I, in contrast, proved with our ham-fisted ineptitude that we were not cut out for armed robberies.

Less than twelve hours later Beniamino had roared out of the port of Livorno, heading briskly for France, where the Druses were expecting him. They would arrange to forward the gold in batches to the various fences and middlemen.

Our French and German accomplices had accompanied him to cover his back, just in case the Lebanese decided to start playing dirty. When there's that much money at stake, people are unpredictable. Missing from the massive shipment of swag was eleven kilograms of finished gold jewelry, about 350 ounces, which we had assigned to other purposes. That was to remain a secret.

There were only three people in town who knew I'd come back. Rudy Scanferla, the one-time manager of La Cuccia, whom I'd greeted with a hug and a fat envelope stuffed with cash and the news that he was about to leave for an extended holiday, and that he would be turning his apartment over to me.

Then Virna, of course. I waited for her in the street outside her apartment. I remembered her saying that when the weather was nice enough, she took Emma for a mid-morning walk. That day there was a pale winter sun.

"Good morning, lovely ladies."

She stared at me, open-mouthed. "Have you come back so they can murder you?"

"If I had, I certainly would be wearing my boots," I replied, pointing to my lace-up suede oxfords. "You know that my will states clearly that I am to be laid to rest in my cowboy boots."

She was smiling again. "I'm not sure I like you like this. You're too different."

"Without my clothes on, I look a lot more like the old Marco."

"Do you feel like a roll in a warm bed with me?"

"Yes, please, as soon as possible."

"How dangerous are you?"

I held out both hands, palms up. "I couldn't say."

She pointed to her daughter, who was trying to grab a teddy bear that was strapped to the stroller. "Come back sometime when you're out of this mess."

I nodded resignedly. "Can I tell you you're beautiful?"

"If we weren't right outside my house, I'd kiss you. I really feel like it."

"So do I."

"Now get out of here."

"Enjoy your walk, my lovely ladies," I said aloud before turning and walking away.

The third person who knew I was back in town was Avvocato Bonotto, and I had an appointment to meet him for lunch that same day. He was a lawyer who had hired me freqently. We both knew that we could trust one another.

We'd arranged to meet for lunch at Donna Irene in Piazzale Pontecorvo. Ubaldo, the owner, used to run a bar that I frequented. He gave me a quick sharp glance as I walked into the place, but if he recognized me, he gave no sign of it. He accompanied me to the table where Bonotto was already comfortably seated, enjoying the wait with a glass of bubbly prosecco.

"Are you the one who needs a lawyer?" he asked.

"No."

"Then why on earth are you dressed in that get-up?"

"I'm trying to avoid certain people."

"Word's going around that . . ."

"That what?"

"That you and your partner were forced to sell La Cuccia and leave town because you sold out one of your customers to the police."

I snickered. "Idle gossip. You believed it?"

"Of course not. I know you better than that. And if you had decided to become a police informer, you would have done it at the time of your choosing."

Ubaldo returned to take our orders. He objected politely but firmly when I ordered a seafood appetizer followed by a veal steak, very rare.

I gave in. "You decide, then."

"Of course I'll decide. And I'll choose the wine as well."

Bonotto laughed heartily but discreetly, and then ran his hand over his snow-white mustache. "Now, what seems to be the problem?"

"The Kosovar Mafiosi of the Peć clan that are operating in Northeast Italy employ only one law firm."

"I'm aware. They work with Antonio Criconia, a colleague here in Padua. He's in the middle of a fairly intricate court case right now."

"It's just more of the usual, coke smuggling on behalf of the spoiled young hipsters and wealthy professionals of this town," I pointed out. "A case that emerges from a lengthy and meticulous investigation . . ."

"So get to the point."

"I want access to the transcripts of the wiretaps and eaves-dropping tapes."

He grasped what I wanted instantly. "So you can find out what they're saying about you and your partner."

"Precisely."

He slipped his fork into the plateful of tagliatelle and spun a mouthful of pasta. "And you'd like me to ask my colleague for this favor?"

"We're willing to pay whatever it takes."

"I'm pretty sure that, when he took on these clients, my colleague had no clear idea of the collateral effects—first and foremost, the fear—involved in becoming a full-time defender on behalf of a certain kind of client."

"He's not the first lawyer to make this kind of mistake."

"Agreed. But my point is this: I doubt that money is enough of an incentive. He has a wife and children."

"We aren't interested in getting him in trouble. We just want to find out what they know about us."

"I can make all kinds of promises, but that's not going to reassure him."

"But he's known you for years."

"True, but we stopped working together a while ago. He knows perfectly well that I disagreed with his professional choices."

"So you're telling me that you won't even try to talk to him?"

"That's right. It would be pointless."

Plan A had failed. Now I had to try Plan B, and I wasn't looking forward to it. I waited for the waitress to take our plates.

"We have to get our hands on those transcripts."

He heaved a deep sigh. "Please, Marco . . . ."

"Look, I don't like this either. It's unpleasant, but this is how matters stand: either he helps us out, or we're going to have to make Avvocato Criconia understand that he has more reason to be afraid of us than of the Kosovars."

"Unpleasant? It's despicable. Do you realize what you're asking me to do?"

I nodded. "We have no alternative."

He got to his feet. "Forgive me if I leave you to your meal. I'm not hungry anymore."

At that point I lost my temper. "If you had any idea what's behind this request, you'd drop this pose of moral superiority."

"I have some sense of professional ethics; you're asking me to deliver a Mafioso extortion message."

"I could write you a *pizzinu* if you like," I badgered him.

He told me to go to hell and left the restaurant. I finished my meal alone, fobbing off the curious waitress with the story that my friend had been urgently summoned back to his law office.

"Before they invented cell phones, people could finish their meals in peace and quiet," she observed.

Without my asking, Ubaldo sent a glass of vintage Calvados over to my table. It was his understated way of letting me know that he'd recognized me. I felt the warm burn of the apple brandy as it moved down my throat and into my belly.

Max la Memoria remained safely ensconced at Fratta Polesine: at the speed that the fat man drove, it was 90 minutes away from Padua, though it took three hours at the speed that ordinary mortals drive. I was waiting for him under the shelter of the porticoes of Piazza dell'Insurrezione, taking care not to wind up in the viewfinder of one of the 120 new videocameras with swiveling lenses and remote zoom that were conveying a live feed of every neighborhood in Padua to the gleaming new command center of the city police.

As usual, a cold wet rain was drumming down. My old leather flight jacket would have kept me warmer than the elegant and expensive overcoat I was wearing that day. A little later a small mob of upright citizens on the hunt for lowlifes came along. They were escorted by a pair of private security gaurds to protect them from the kids from the social centers who used to kick their asses whenever they ran into them. They saw me from a distance and headed straight for me. As they drew closer, they noticed the color of my skin and my expensive clothing. They changed course and headed on down the porticoes. As they went by, the man who must have been their leader greeted me in a low voice and gave me a look, hoping to receive a white Italian citizen's gratitude for their protection. I pretended to be intent on my cell phone. They were the last thing I needed.

Every corner of Padua was being patrolled by patrols and "megapatrols," as the newspapers had come to dub them, and there were uniforms of every description.

With the ostensible goal of freeing the city's neighborhoods of pushers and whores, in reality the vigilante patrols were so many campaign promises being kept, as well as placeholders, doing advance groundwork for the witch-hunt that was in the offing. As soon as the security bill now making its way through Italian parliament was approved, hunting season would be open and the vigilantes would be off.

And the biggest supporters of that law were, of course, Mafiosi of every nationality. They would finally be able to rid the cities of their annoying competitors, unaffiliated small-time crooks, the annoying freelance criminals who wound up in the newspapers on a daily basis, threatening to upset their profitable and discreet arrangements.

In the meantime, the law-abiding citizens of Northeast Italy continued to entrust their elderly relatives to illegal-immigrant nurses and caregivers; their houses were still being cleaned and their meals were being cooked by undocumented housekeepers. Workshops, factories, construction yards, new highways, and shipyards were all staffed by illegal immigrants who had made their way across Italy's porous borders locked up in 40-foot containers or aboard rusty and terrifyingly dangerous old freighters. An underpaid, easily extorted labor force that could simply be expelled from the country if they caused trouble or made demands—without even having to invoke the usual excuses of a slowing economy or rocketing inflation. And those same upright citizens continued exploiting for their sexual gratification Nigerian prostitutes and Brazilian transexuals, young women and underage boys from every country in the old East European bloc.

Simple arithmetic told you that more than a few people had to be preaching one thing and practicing quite another, on the one hand braying about clean streets and law and order, and on the other hand shamelessly exploiting the illegals.

In Northeast Italy, for that matter, unprincipled cynics were in charge. More than before. More than ever before. The owners of little factories and businessmen with luxury cars, elegant villas, and millions invested overseas who had never paid a lira or a euro in taxes in their lives. Waste disposal tycoons who exported thousands of tons of toxic plastic to China, plastic that was then recycled into brand-new toys for children around the world. And there were pillars of the community in the same sector who obliged women who had immigrated illegally from third-world countries to sort through garbage bare-handed.

To say nothing of call centers where dozens of Italian women worked only to be paid under the counter, waiting months at a time for their wages, and never uttering a word of complaint because, with unemployed husbands and children to feed, a job—however crappy—was still a job.

To say nothing of the entrepreneurs who ran websites listing young escorts, and who were always eager to buy the houses where the women entertained their clients, because real estate is always the best investment, even during a recession.

To say nothing of politicians and public officials who kept taking the same bribes they'd always taken, but now they camouflaged them with consulting fees and agreements and, in the rare occasions when they were caught, they hastened to state that it had been a "single episode of weakness" . . . But the truth was quite different: illegal machinations were the order of the day in every sector of hard-working Northeast Italy, and it had become a fertile terrain for organized crime of every kind to take root. The mafias of the world had sunk their teeth into the Northeast, and nothing would stop them from eating to their heart's delight. Money laundering had become the meeting ground between unprincipled cynics and Mafiosi. Only politicians, and with them the local press and television, continued to pretend not to notice that this was the part of Italy that had the highest concentration of organized crime. And they weren't pretending for their political futures alone, because if there is one thing that the mafias of the world understood long ago, it's that the only way to do real business is to be on good terms with everyone—absolutely everyone.

And the respectable citizens and voters were all happy to bray for the heads of the illegal immigrants because everything else, the really bad stuff, all things considered, was going splendidly. The mafia money made the wheels spin round, business was booming, and there was a positive synergy with legal businesses of all kinds. Even more effective than the nocturnal patrols of those gentlemen wearing phosphorescent bibs were the police cars stationed outside the clinics that offered medical care "even" to illegal immigrants. It had become common practice in many different cities and towns in the province of Padua, and fear had begun to spread among the poor, the sick, and the vulnerable.

Max appeared at my side. "And here I am."

"You're late," I scolded him as we walked across the piazza.

"Twelve minutes late. When it's raining I tend to lower my maximum velocity."

"It's dangerous to drive 35 mph on a superhighway. There's a good chance that a Greek or Bulgarian truck driver who's been powering cross-country for ten hours without a rest might rear-end you."

"Are you in a bad mood?"

"I'm worried that the past two years in Switzerland haven't

been good for me. I can't wrap my head around the idea that this fucking Northeast Italy I've always lived in is becoming unlivable."

"So you're looking around and you don't like what you see, eh?"

"It's worse. I think, I analyze, and I find everything morally intolerable."

"Yup, it's a mess. You need to purge your system and come back and live with us cynical assholes."

"That won't be easy."

"One week of drinking spritz in the piazza cafés and you'll see how easy it is."

We'd arrived at the street entrance of the office building that housed Avvocato Criconia's law firm. "Can you imagine me showing up for an aperitif dressed like this?"

"For once you'd be dressed like everyone else; you could finally extend your circle of acquaintances. The next step is Facebook, but I'll explain that to you some other time."

The lawyer was a man of average height, skinny, with a face that made you think of a turtle wearing a toupee. He might have been a little older than sixty. He opened the door for us, but he carefully avoided greeting us. We'd hurt his feelings by threatening him, but we overlooked his wounded emotions. We followed him into the library, where there were ten or so thick files waiting for us on a conference table.

"I'll be in my office. Let me know when you've finished."

The transcriptions of the wiretaps and other electronic monitoring involved an investigation into a coke ring that was servicing a number of socialites who frequented certain exclusive clubs and other facilities in the center of Padua and in the hillside homes up on the Colli Euganei. The Carabinieri were able to blackmail one of their informants into placing hidden microphones all over the place; now they knew that it was the Kosovars who were dealing the Colombian coke.

Max snickered with satisfaction as he read through the list of names. "Lookee lookee, all the respectable citizens."

We weren't interested in the converstions of the highly placed coke addicts; we wanted to see what the Kosovars had to say. We started reading through their conversations, in translation, and found only one reference to us. In a conversation caught by a hidden mike, a certain Lenez, newly arrived from Peć, asked an accomplice named Arben Alshabani (who was an ambitious second-tier capo according to a Carabinieri report) if there was any news concerning the friends of the "bellydancer's man." Arben told him that they had left town and no one knew where they had gone, adding that it was annoying to have to go after people without knowing the reason why; it's the kind of situation in which you make mistakes that can prove dangerous, even fatal.

Lenez had gently reminded him that he wasn't important enough to have to know everything. Arben had shot back that maybe he would be too busy to have time to look for those guys, and Lenez had brusquely snapped an expression that the translator had rendered: "Do whatever the fuck you think best."

Then they'd started on a new topic: the internal feuding in the family. Both Lenez and Arben were second cousins of the late Fatjon Bytyçi. According to Lenez, the patriarch and boss of the Peć clan was saddened at the death of his oldest son, but not distraught. He had always preferred Fatjon's younger brother Agim, who was much smarter, more capable, and who had leadership qualities, as he had shown in the years when he commanded a KLA unit.

"Why do Mafiosi always seem to have one useless son?"

The fat man gave me a baffled glance. "You've lost me there."

"Take *The Godfather*. Fredo, Don Vito Corleone's second-born son, is a pervert and is turning into an informer. Michael has to have him killed. Or A.J. Soprano, Tony Soprano's only son: he's an ineffectual mess, and he even tries to kill himself."

"So are you just running off at the mouth, or should I try to make sense of this?"

"Don't try too hard, I can help you. It seems obvious to me that the Bytyçi clan doesn't want people to figure out how that sicko Fatjon really died."

"And so?"

"So up till now, before I read these transcriptions, I thought that we were in much worse trouble than we seem to be. I figured that the old boss got up every morning and asked whether we had been killed yet. Instead, it looks like we're far from a top priority for him, seeing that he hasn't given Arben a kick in the ass, even though Arben's clearly uninterested in tracking us down."

"You can rest assured though that if we ever fall into their hands they'll slice us up into catfood, just to make it clear to everyone that you can't touch a Bytyçi."

"Maybe so. But it strikes me that we have an opportunity to take advantage of how embarrassed they are about Fatjon's perversions."

"Okay, but let's start by finding out the official version of his murder. There's nothing about that here. This Arben is very careful not to spell things out. It's probably no accident that, even though the police are sure that he's an important clan underboss, they still haven't been able to issue a warrant for his arrest."

Max la Memoria copied down names and took notes in his notebook with his clear and minute handwriting. I killed time looking out the window and smoking.

When we told the lawyer that we were done, he didn't even bother to look up from the file he was reading.

It pissed me off. "Have they already asked you to smuggle a cell phone into prison?"

He looked up and glared at me contemptuously.

"When they do, remember, you won't be able to say no."

The fat man tugged at my sleeve. "Forget about him, what do you care?"

"Arrogant shit."

"Nowadays, every successful lawyer is arrogant. They have to be. He'll be disbarred otherwise."

"What the fuck are you talking about?"

"What the fuck are *you* talking about? You're starting to sound like one of these little altarboy opposition politicos."

"You really think so?" I asked, deeply concerned.

"You need to drink more and you need to get more pussy. Hurry, it's not too late."

The discovery that killing me was not a top priority for the Kosovar mafia made me feel confident enough to lower my security restrictions. I went to the Anfora for an aperitif. Before walking in the door, I took off my sunglasses and my tie. I was immediately hailed by Alberto and a number of the regulars; there was a blizzard of wisecracks about my prolonged absence, and they quickly brought me up to date with all the news about our old friends. I stayed for dinner and then went back to Scanferla's grim little apartment, intending to catch a quick nap until it was time for the evening spritz.

But in the middle of the afternoon the doorbell woke me up. A short ring, followed by a pause, and then two more rings. Rossini was back. He was dragging a wheeled suitcase that looked like it was very heavy.

"Don't tell me you've got all our money in that suitcase."

"I haven't had time to go to the bank yet." He looked around, and then pointed at the bed. "That's the only one, isn't it?"

"There's a couch."

"We couldn't find anything better?"

"We're going to have to make do."

He grunted in disappointment. As he was taking off his coat and pants, I brought him up to speed on the latest developments. Then he grabbed a blanket, lay down on the couch, and fell asleep.

Once again, I felt a surge of envy. All he had to do was lay his head on a pillow and he dropped into a deep sleep. I always had to watch hours of television shopping shows to knock myself out. I thought to myself that sooner or later I was going to have to seriously consider breaking myself of the habit.

I made a cup of coffee and smoked a couple of cigarettes. Then I left the apartment and walked toward the center of Padua. I windowshopped and killed time until the bars, the piazzas, and the surrounding streets began to fill up with people. That was when I started looking for Morena Borromeo.

I finally found her in Piazza delle Erbe, smoking with a couple of her girlfriends, warming themselves by a freestanding patio heater. They were all three dressed identically, made up identically, and their hairdos were identical as well. The police informer was older than the other two, who couldn't have been over thirty.

When I walked up to them, all three turned to me with the same professional escort smile, telegraphing that they were free for the evening. But when Morena recognized me, her face changed expression. She seemed genuinely pleased to see me. She got rid of her friends with a brusque goodbye and gave me a hug.

"I haven't seen you around for a while."

"I had a lot of vacation time I needed to use up."

"I haven't thanked you yet for putting that bastard in his place."

"I have no idea what you're talking about."

"Fine, fine, message received," she whispered. "I see you've finally started dressing like a little gentleman."

"A drink and dinner?"

"Sure, and after-dinner if you want. But the meter's already running."

"So you finally decided to get a boss."

She sipped her spritz. "It's an agency, not a pimp. They only take a percentage of my time keeping company in public. The money for the tricks I get to keep."

I observed her carefully. She still looked great, though another couple of years of cocaine had left their mark. She began playing her part. I let her work without interrupting. I needed time to figure out if she was still in the informant business.

We moved to another bar, and stayed there until she got hungry.

"Now let me take you to a brand new place: cozy, unusual, and . . . expensive."

"As long as it's not one of your cokehead restaurants. I don't want to eat in a place where dealers are selling drugs from table to table."

"Relax. The place looks fake, it's such an elite crowd. But the food is incredibly good."

The place looked like an old downtown *osteria*, only with fine crystal, designer silverware, and five-star food presentation. The dishes all had the kinds of names that evoke spectacular crescendos of flavors, the names that food journalists seem to swoon over. In reality, though, the meal was just a grab-bag of flavors that, given the money we were paying, we couldn't afford not to enjoy.

But there was another reason that you couldn't have persuaded me to go back to that restaurant. Everyone was talking in low, hushed voices; no one laughed out loud; the waiters came and went as silently as ghosts. It was a restaurant frequented by well-mannered corpses.

"You still dating your handsome policeman?"

"Last year his wife left him, so now he fucks me on a regular basis. Every Sunday. He shows up with a gift-wrapped tray of pastries, after taking his children to Mass, and he goes at it till late at night."

"So you're his girlfriend now?"

"Well, in a way. He treats me a little better, he tells me things. Typical male: he can't wrap his head around the fact that his wife finally dumped him."

"And you're happy with how things are going?"

"I can't complain."

"How much do you take home at the end of the month?"

"Three thousand euros, after taxes, but I don't usually talk about that with my customers."

"Maybe it would be worth talking about with me."

She smiled. "I was just starting to wonder when you'd get around to telling me the real reason for this nostalgic get-together."

"Do you think you could get your cop to do a little work for me?"

She ran a breadstick over her lips before taking a tiny bite. "Are you looking to cut me out?"

"No. I'll need you to keep an eye on him and warn me if he's planning to fuck me."

"What's in it for me?"

"A year's income."

"What about my bonuses?"

"Forty thousand euros. Not a euro more."

"And how much is he going to get?"

"More than you get, of course, but it's a separate deal."

She stared at me. "Maybe you're not offering me enough money."

"Don't be greedy. He's not the only crooked cop in town."

"Okay. I'll talk to him."

I seized her hand. I wanted to make sure that she realized how serious I was. "In this movie, traitors die."

"Are you trying to scare me?"

"I'm trying to make you understand something."

"Does this have anything to do with that old drug heist?"

"No," I lied.

"Do you remember that my handsome policeman was monitoring the phone calls of cops in another jurisdiction who were suspected of being responsible for the heist?"

"Vaguely."

"It was them, all right, but all the tapes with the recordings of the wiretaps were mysteriously demagnetized, and the investigation was archived."

These are things that happen when the intelligence services are involved, I thought to myself, but all I said to her was: "See what happens when you rely on technology?"

"My cop told me that his higher-ups never really intended to take those other cops to court."

"Then why spy on them?"

"I asked him the same thing, but I didn't understand the answer: 'Reselling it wasn't part of the agreement, it was an excess of zeal and a lack of communication'."

Then, as if nothing had happened, she resumed her performance, acting the part of the woman that you absolutely have to take to bed. After a while, she realized how ridiculous it was and began making fun of herself. We both burst into laughter, attracting the attention of the living dead who were dining at the other tables around us.

"Tonight, it's on the house."

"I'm not sure I'm up for it."

"Come have a glass of something at my house and let's see what happens."

Later, in her apartment, while Morena was preparing a line of coke for herself, I started snooping around in her collection of CDs, just to avoid standing there like an idiot staring at her. I was surprised to discover an Alberta Adams CD, *Born with the Blues*. It must have just wound up there by chance.

Edoardo "Catfish" Fassio had introduced me to Alberta. I

was immediately enchanted by her voice: the voice of an attrac-
tively jazzed-up 77-year-old woman with an incredible charge
of vitality.

After starting her career in Detroit nightclubs at the end of
the Thirties, and after going through a number of unsuccessful
marriages, she had decided to go back into the recording studio
not once but four different times when others her age were
griping about their arthritis.

I slipped the CD into the player and chose my favorite song,
Searchin'. I closed my eyes. It didn't take Alberta long to convince me that making love that night might not be a bad idea at
all. I took off my jacket and began loosening my tie.

It was just before lunch when I got back to my apartment.
My host wasn't an early riser, and no one left her bed before
eleven, just in time to head out for the first aperitif of the day.

"I'm in a hurry to meet your handsome policeman," I
reminded her as I planted a kiss on her cheek.

"You get your money ready, and you'll meet him tonight."

Max was cooking; he looked questioningly at me. Beniamino, instead, came over to me and took a deep, stage sniff.

He turned to the fat man. "I hereby announce that he
screwed Snow White's evil stepmother."

"Yikes," Max commented as he stirred the risotto.

They began to rib me mercilessly. I got sick of it after awhile.

"Most likely I'm going to meet with the cop this evening."

Rossini's face became serious. "That's good news."

Max la Memoria went on with the ribbing. "Excellent. That
means we'll overlook your strange perversions and we'll allow
you to share our humble meal."

The handsome policeman had a name and a surname: Attilio
Carini. He picked me up in front of the train station a little after
one in the morning and gestured for me to remain silent. He

drove up onto an overpass, sped through an entire section of town, and turned onto the ramp that led onto the ring highway around town.

He was somewhere between forty-five and fifty years old, physically fit, with an alert face set off by a perfectly bald head. He dressed unostentatiously—no designer clothes, no expensive watches. He drove at moderate speed, and the unnecessary miles he drove had a very clear purpose behind them: he wanted to give me the time to consider carefully just what kind of cop he was so that our conversation could get off on the right foot. I gradually came to the conclusion that he was not corrupt in the classical sense of that word, because he wasn't allied with the bad guys. If he ever took money, he would do so only once he was certain that to do so would harm neither an ongoing investigation nor any of his fellow policemen. He wasn't the kind of bad cop who acts recklessly just to service a vice or to keep a mistress.

I found myself obliged to come up with a very different strategy from the one I'd agreed on earlier that day with my friends.

He stopped the car in a highway pullout and gestured for me to get out. He frisked me carefully for microphones or recording devices.

"Now it's my turn," I said once he'd finished searching me.

"You must be kidding me!" he snarled.

"If you won't let me check, it means you're wearing a wire."

He shrugged and raised his arms. I did just as meticulous a search as he had, and then I demanded that we leave both our cell phones in the warmth of the car and step about fifty feet away from the vehicle. I'd heard about a guy who was screwed for having had a conversation a little too close to a car bumper.

"All right, let's get to the point," he said as he lit a cigarette.

"Do you know who I am?"

"What kind of an amateur do you take me for?"

"Well, I just wanted to make sure that I don't need to introduce myself."

"No, there's no need of that. So what do you want from me?"

"I want to fuck a Serbian gang that operates in Northeast Italy. The local boss is called Pavle Stojkovic and he's working with a woman, possibly German, called Greta Gardner."

"In my line of work the verb 'fuck' can have a lot of different meanings."

"True. As far I'm concerned, we're not talking about physically eliminating anyone. I just want to dismantle the organization."

"So what do you want from me?"

"Useful information."

"You should be the one giving information to me. I'd be sure to pass it on to my colleagues with proper jurisdiction."

"Let's not waste time kidding each other. There's 100,000 euros in it for you and, if you're interested, a bonus: you get to catch them with their hands in the honey pot."

"Honey that I'll bet you'll be supplying."

"Oh yes. Plenty of shiny, sticky honey . . . Some might even stick to the fingers of whoever finds it."

"So what you're saying is that you want the police to take them out of circulation for you?"

"It's the deal of a lifetime: you get money and a career boost."

"That might be something I'm interested in."

"Except?"

"Except I have to be sure that this whole operation isn't just one gang getting another gang out of the way."

"They fucked with the wrong woman, and someone's pissed. That's all."

"Are you asking me to believe that?"

"I've never been more serious in my life."

He offered me a cigarette. "Speaking of women. You'd be giving the 100,000 euros to Morena."

"Right. So no one can link the money to you."

"That's not the only reason. That money's for her."

"So why are you telling me about it?"

"Morena is going to turn over a new leaf. No more coke, no more cocks."

"Does she know about it?"

"Not yet. But now you do. So keep your hands out of her panties."

We got back in the car and said as little during the ride back as we had on the ride out. So the handsome policeman was sick of the loneliness of divorce and had decided to make an honest woman of Morena. It wasn't a bad idea. She was on the verge of becoming too old for her business. Another couple of years, and she'd have to cut her rates drastically. When it comes to turning tricks, you can't beat youth.

He dropped me off at the station, where my friends were waiting for me in a Japanese-made car with unusual lines. The car was black, with tinted windows. I got in back and made a disgruntled noise. "This is nice and inconspicuous."

If one day I was able to go back to my old life, the first thing I'd do was get my old Skoda Felicia, currently in the loving care of Paolo Valentini.

"He saw it, and there was no way to stop him," the fat man told me. "He wouldn't even bargain on the price; he pretended to believe that it really has just 1,200 miles on the odometer."

Beniamino stroked the steering wheel lovingly. "It's sort of like a scale model of a mid-century American car."

"You mean the cars that drove around Chicago full of gangsters with a tommy gun in their lap?"

"Well, the cars from the movies of my childhood. Masterpieces: *A Touch of Evil* or *Asphalt Jungle*. The first one taught me how to deal with cops; the second taught me how not to split up the take from a robbery."

"Don't you want to know how it went with the cop?"

"It went fine," said Old Rossini. "Otherwise you'd never have busted my chops about the car."

I looked out the window and realized we weren't heading for Scanferla's apartment. When it dawned on me that we were in my old neighborhood I asked where we were going.

"We have a decent place to stay now," Max replied. "You can call Rudy and tell him he can go back to his rathole."

A cluster of gleaming new apartment buildings stood where there was once only countryside and I rode bicycles with small armies of boys my age.

The apartment was big and fully furnished. Each of us would have his own room.

"Nice place," I commented.

"They're going to rent it out as a pied-à-terre for visiting managers of a multinational corporation. It's costing us about what a villa on the Costa Smeralda costs in August."

Beniamino patted his wheeled suitcase packed with cash. "Don't quibble about money, boys. At my age, I need comfort and cleanliness."

The fat man was hungry, and he suggested having a plate of pasta. I sat in the kitchen to keep him company while he busied himself at the stove. Rossini withdrew into his bedroom to make an international phone call to Sylvie. He came back with a worried look on his face.

"I don't feel comfortable being so far away from her," he explained, nervously fingering the bracelets that dangled from his wrist. "If I'm not there, she doesn't like to go out, and spending all her time indoors isn't good for her."

"But there's always someone with her to protect her, right?"

"Two trusted bodyguards stay with her everywhere she goes. It's a pretty big slice of the family budget."

"How does she spend her days, now that she's given up dancing?"

"Mornings she works at a rape crisis center. Once a week she sees a shrink, then I take her shopping and in the evenings we go to the best nightclubs in the city. The real problem is the night. In the old days, she lived for the night. Now it's become a nightmare that never ends."

Max served out platefuls of pasta and asked me to open a bottle of wine. The old old smuggler seemed to be lost in a reverie. He ate a couple of forkfuls of pasta before continuing. "For the first time in my life, I'm sure that payback isn't going to change a thing. Killing the person that decided to take her to that gang bang parlor isn't going to help Sylvie at all."

"You just have to hope for the best. Time helps."

He waved one hand in the air resignedly. "No, she'll never be happy the way she was. She's not my dancer anymore. Those bastards killed her in Corenc. And that's why I'm going to kill them. It's vengeance for a woman who no longer exists."

Things had changed in the police stations of Italy. A policeman couldn't surf the criminal databases for information without leaving a trace anymore. Carini must necessarily have asked a superior officer for authorization to delve into information on the Serbs. As I clutched the thin file tight, I wondered if he'd mentioned my name. He'd probably just used the usual excuse of an informant, but by then it didn't really matter anymore. Each of us would play the game according to his own rules and neither would be sticklers about regulations. In the game we were playing, what mattered was to know when to stop, to avoid getting hurt needlessly.

Morena was glowing with happiness when we made the exchange in a large downtown bookstore. Money for information.

"Oh, money just smells so good," she chirped in a little-girl voice.

"Remember our agreement," I said as I handed her a folded sheet of paper with the number of my new cell phone. "You stick to your handsome policeman's ass like a deer tick, and if you have the slightest suspicion that he's planning to fuck me . . ."

"I sound the alarm. The concept is clear to me."

"Good."

She pulled out the Alberta Adams CD. "I brought you a present."

"Thanks."

"Maybe when you listen to it you'll think of me sometimes."

"I didn't think you were so romantic."

"I would have preferred someone like you," she whispered. "Someone who doesn't lecture you, someone who never thinks about today, tomorrow, and all that. But at a certain point, a girl has to choose, right?"

"You need a guy like him. There's no future with a guy like me."

She took off one glove and stroked my cheek, her eyes glistening.

"I liked you better when you were being the irresistible woman with the heart of stone. That was more exciting."

She turned on her heel and, muttering an insult, stomped out. I was baffled. I didn't think I'd said anything offensive, but I sure wasn't going to talk it over with my friends. They didn't like Morena, and they'd almost certainly find a reason to point out yet again that I didn't understand a thing about women.

It was raining, as usual. We hadn't seen a winter like this in years. It had even snowed once or twice. I opened my umbrella and hurried toward the streetcar stop. I'd get off after just three stops, but I took the streetcar to make sure that no one was following me. I didn't want to be the one to blow our comfortable hideout. That same morning, Rossini had gone to pick up a nice little "armory" from a delicatessen owner; the guy had inherited two businesses from his father—the deli and a side business of providing weapons for armed robbery teams. Max, on the other hand, was in charge of procuring cloned cell phones and other diabolical electronic devices. If the police searched the apartment, there was everything they'd need to send all three of us to jail for several years.

I hopped off the streetcar at the very next stop, and flagged a taxi. After a short cab ride, I took a bus. The last stretch of road I walked.

Beniamino had scattered pieces of pistol all over the table in the living room. He was cleaning and oiling the guns very intently.

"Those look like antiques," I mocked.

"Don't be sacrilegious. They're two solid and workmanlike Colt .45's. They've been satisfying connoisseurs since 1911."

"He's a gun fetishist," Max laughed. "For instance, he loves the guns that Bruce Willis uses in *Last Man Standing*. A few years ago he made me watch that movie, twice, on DVD."

"Okay then, we're safe. Bruce never loses."

"You can be sure of that, boy," Rossini snapped in annoyance.

I pulled the file out of the envelope and laid it on the table, next to a box of bullets. "When you're done playing with your toys we can take a look at this."

"Just give me a minute to reassemble them. Which I could do blindfolded, if necessary."

Less than two minutes. Confident, precise movements. The prospect of Rossini armed reassured his friends and unsettled his enemies. My jokes were just a way of concealing my nervousness. I didn't like guns, but I knew we needed them. Both Max and I were willing to let Rossini handle the weapons. And get his hands dirty.

The fat man pulled off the blue rubberband and opened the file. The first sheet was blank, expect for a single line at the top of the page.

It was about Greta Gardner: "Unknown."

Concerning Pavle Stojkovic, there was an abundance of information, though wherever the name of an Italian policeman appeared it had been blocked out in heavy black marker. The biographical section noted that he had been born in Kladovo, eastern Serbia, in May 1950. In 1972 in Belgrade he had married Ivana, the following year Bratislav was born; his second-born was a daughter, Sonja, born in 1980. At the time, Pavle was already a high-ranking officer in the UDBA, the Yugoslavian intelligence service. When the secret police organization was disbanded in the wake of the civil war, he took a post in an unidentified office in the Serbian Defense Ministry.

In the mid-Nineties he had become a consigliere of a criminal family in the capital that then clashed with the crime family of Zeljko Raznatovic, better known as Arkan, the Tiger of the Balkans, and was decimated. Somehow, Pavle miraculously survived the slaughter of the gang chiefs and the mass desertion of the footsoldiers and made his way into hiding. He reappeared in Italy in the spring of 2000, just a few months after the murder of Arkan in the lobby of the Intercontinental Hotel in Belgrade.

He'd been given an Italian visa on a special expedited basis at the request of an official in the Italian Foreign Ministry whose name was obliterated by a thick layer of black ink. Perhaps it was as payment for information secretly provided to the investigators working for the International Criminal Tribunal of the Hague, who were gathering evidence to indict and arrest Slobodan Milosevic, facing charges of crimes against humanity.

In 2001, immediately following the arrest of the former president of Yugoslavia, Stojkovic had founded the Balkan Market, with headquarters in Treviso, the usual import-export company with just two employees: Bozidar Dinic and Vladan Ninkovic.

"Look at them, Hans and Fritz," I joked. "The bastard even gave his musclemen health insurance."

Max tapped his index finger on another sheet of paper. "This is a note from the police headquarters of Treviso: it says that our friend Pavle is a good guy and nobody should bother him."

I stubbed out what was left of my cigarette in the ashtray. "That means that the exchanges of favors continued over time, and that Pavle is more than just a gangster."

"Then why are they letting us fuck him now?" asked Rossini.

"Hard to say," the fat man replied. "Maybe he's not so useful anymore as an informer; maybe the cops in Padua couldn't care less about deals made with him by other cops . . ."

I felt like having a drink, but I looked at the clock and decided to tough it out. "So now we know a lot more about our boy Pavle. But I don't think we have anything useful for planning out a clear strategy."

"In fact, we do seem to have run out of ideas," the fat man admitted. "Either we charge in with our eyes closed and see what happens or we wait until we have more information."

Rossini jangled his bracelets. "The longer we wait, the easier we are to spot. And once they identify us, they'll attack us."

"So what's our first move?"

The fat man thought about it through one long drag on his cigarette and then, exhaling, looked at me. "It's your turn. You're going to go have a chat with Arben Alshabani; we'll cover your back."

At ten sharp that evening I pulled open the door of the bar and was engulfed in a flood of heat and the stench of tobacco. In that bar, at least, officially owned by a pair of Moroccan sisters, the law against smoking indoors was not being observed—they evidently figured that if certain people want to get cancer, it's the least of their problems. I looked around me. Seated at the café tables were representatives of all the specialties of low-level criminal endeavor.

The two sisters were both standing behind the bar, and they were chatting animatedly with a number of customers who were deeply involved in their beers and their panini. True to the classic script directions, no one looked up. I sat down at the one unoccupied table. Given its privileged location, it must have been Alshabani's usual perch, but there was no sign of the ambitious underboss. To keep from collapsing from the heat, I took off my overcoat and got comfortable at the table. After a few minutes, the younger of the two presumptive owners came over and asked what I'd be having. I ordered an espresso.

I knew that Arben was somewhere in the back, and that he was watching me, ready to duck out the back door if things started looking bad. I pulled a folded-up newspaper out of my pocket and began reading, making a brave pretense of interest in the ongoing political debate within the minority center-right coalition over its inability to agree on an acceptable candidate to run for the office of mayor.

In reality I was just trying to appear relaxed so that I could conquer the Kosovar's mistrust. Mafiosi are mistrustful by nature. When they wake up every morning the first thing they think about it is how to go out and screw their neighbor, taking special care to sniff out the slightest risk to themselves of falling into the same trap: if they get ripped off, it can lead to a dangerous and uncontrollable drop in their popularity within the shark-infested social network of their crime family. In that sense they lead a difficult life, there's never a time when they can relax: the real danger is much more likely to come from within than from outside enemies. You never know: one day, without thinking about it, you could say the wrong word at the wrong time, or you could fail to run your businesses as successfully as expected. And when that happens, a slow but ineluctable mechanism begins to operate, relegating you forever at the lowest ranks of your organization. True enough, this can happen in any ordinary corporation. But there, if you're young enough, you can always quit and go look for another job: that's not possible in the mafia.

The Kosovar Arben was fully steeped in this general logic—in fact, he embraced it and wallowed in it. As the Carabinieri had correctly surmised, he was ambitious and he wanted to climb rapidly to the highest levels of the criminal organization. His ultimate goal, according to our interpretation of the ambiguous eavesdropping transcripts that we'd been allowed to read in the law offices of Avvocato Criconia, was to replace Florian Tuda, who was in charge of the family operations in Padua. And he'd had some success in that direction: Florian had been arrested during the police sweep that had "deci-mated" the cocaine dealers who supplied one of the many rings in the more prosperous circles of Padua. That was hardly the end of Florian though: in the mafia, bosses can easily run oper-ations from a jail cell, and Arben could do no more than to flaunt the same prerogatives of power as Tuda.

The organizational strategy of the Kosovars was to absorb existing structures and to control them from behind the scenes. In the city of Padua they had focused on taking over bars and clubs run by the Maghrebi underworld, like the bar I was sit-ting in pretending to read a newspaper. The sub-Saharan north Africans had been the first generation of foreign organized crime in Padua, and now they had been reduced to the status of messenger boys given their intractable internal divisions and their reluctance to engage in armed warfare.

The day before, under the porticoes of Via San Francesco, we had slipped a couple of banknotes to Morched the Tunisian, trusted purveyor of hashish to Max la Memoria. In exchange, he had explained to us that the Moroccans and the Algerians weren't pleased with the way things had wound up, and they were planning an insanely reckless move: they wanted to go into business on their own. One of the reasons for their discontent was the heavyhanded approach employed by Arben Alshabani. He would have his enforcers beat street peddlers bloody for the slightest infraction of his rigid rules.

The Kosovar was a perfect model of the kind of Mafioso we'd all had an opportunity to get to know, especially during our stays in Italy's prisons. He was the most predictable kind, because he was stupid, even though he considered himself to be damned clever. With people like him, we'd always managed to get the upper hand, and that was why we'd organized this meeting via Morched.

"We thought we could bring you into a deal we're looking at," the fat man had explained.

The Tunisian eyed us suspiciously. A pair of dark and furtive eyes peered out at us from the depths of the enormous hood of his parka. The rightful owner of that jacket must have been at least three sizes bigger than Morched.

"Either you guys are in trouble or you're trying to pull something. I don't have any pull anymore. It's not like in the old days, when everyone spoke respectfully to Morched when there was something to be resolved . . ."

Max raised a hand to halt the flow of words. "Spare us your tale of woe about your career as a pusher. We just want to get in touch with Arben."

"You're looking to rip him off. His people will cut my throat."

"No. We're just looking to offer him a deal, and you'll be a thousand euros richer for it."

Morched rubbed his hands together vigorously. He was still wary, but the money was tempting. "What would I have to do?"

"Go talk to him and tell him that someone you know and trust . . ."

"Which would be you?"

The fat man pointed at me.

"I don't know him well. I want 1,200 euros."

Beniamino gestured angrily, irritated at the interruption. "You need to shut up and listen."

"Hey, take it easy. Can't a person negotiate anymore? I tell you, the old ways are dying out."

"Fine, 1,200 euros," Max broke in. "But my friend has a point. You need to listen now."

Morched pretended to zip his mouth shut.

"You'll go to Arben and tell him that a guy you know, Marco Buratti, gave you five thousand euros to buy heroin and cocaine from various suppliers just to test the quality, because he's planning to buy a couple of kilos of shit."

The dealer nodded. "So he'll want to know more and agree to meet the buyer in person."

"I can see that you catch on fast."

"There's better people than Arben in Padua."

"You mean there are people who are more generous to you than Arben . . . but I only want to deal with him."

Morched held out his hand, open-palmed, to get the money. "Fine, but don't come complaining to me when Alshabani rips you off."

I methodically counted out the bills and on an old bus ticket I'd written a phone number. "Tell the Kosovar that I'll only agree to meetings in a public place."

Beniamino had opened his overcoat and let Morched catch a glimpse of the two handguns in the underarm holsters. "I know that times are tough, and five thousand euros is a lot of cash, but if you steal them, or you say the wrong things, I will find you and so help me, I'll kill you."

Morched turned toward the fat man. "Have I ever robbed you or disappointed you, friend?"

"No, and that's why we gave you the money in advance. But up till now I've never done a deal for more than two or three hundred euros with you, and maybe you assume that we're just a bunch of fools."

The Tunisian threw his arms out in a pose of wounded innocence.

"What kind of world are we living in? You can't negotiate, you get beaten up, and people threaten to kill you for no good reason. And you know whose fault it really is? It's your fault. If you Italians hadn't opened your eastern borders none of this would have happened. Those are bad people, and they're only going to spoil everything, but you wanted them in at all costs."

"Tell the Kosovar only about me. You never saw my friends."

"You know, you're very complicated, you people? I'm not sure I'd like to work with you guys," and he wandered off, muttering and gesticulating.

"Did you really have to threaten him?" I asked Rossini as we walked back to the car.

"Maybe not, but he's a failed gangster, and he's living in the past."

"And he's a pusher," I thought, remembering how the old smuggler hated drug dealers. In any case, Morched did what he'd been paid to do, and he called me two hours later. A meeting with Arben was scheduled for the morning of the following day in the bar in the Piazza Mazzini where I sat waiting for his majesty Alshabani to deign to come out and talk with me.

I raised my hand and signaled to one of the two Moroccan women to come over; she slowly came out from behind the bar and with some evident annoyance strolled over to my table. I pointed to the door to the back, where a scuffed-up old sign warned that the customers could not enter.

"I know that Arben is in there. Tell him that I'm leaving in two minutes."

"Why don't you go in the bathroom and take a piss? Maybe when you come out he'll be here waiting for you."

The Kosovar wanted to make sure I wasn't wearing a microphone, but stepping into the bathroom could mean a knife to the chest or a bullet to the head. The minute the Tunisian said my name, Arben must have remembered the death sentence that hung over my head.

I shook my head. "Two minutes and I'm out of here," I repeated decisively.

The woman disappeared behind the door. I stood up and took off my jacket. Standing in shirtsleeves, I removed the battery from my cell phone. I could still be hiding a tiny listening device somewhere on my body, but it struck me as a gesture of goodwill. Apparently, that's how Arben took it. He finally decided to emerge from concealment.

I found myself in the presence of a man who was pretty different from the one I'd seen in the surveillance photographs.

His hair wasn't cropped short anymore, the way most ex-KLA men wore it. Now he wore his hair long, shoulder-length, and he looked younger than thirty-six, the age provided in the notes from his defense lawyer. His close-set eyes and his thin but prominent nose gave him a less than intelligent appearance, but from the way he looked at me I could see I was dealing with someone I should take care not to underestimate.

I glimpsed a flash of cunning in his gaze; it told me that Arben had earned his position as underboss in the field. First in Kosovo, in anti-Serb guerrilla warfare, and later in the family company. He was a cunning, violent guy. I needed to convince him that he could screw me anytime he wanted.

He shook hands and flashed a hearty smile. He turned toward the bar and ordered a beer. The beer was served at blinding speed.

"Morched told me that you're interested in buying certain merchandise," he began in a conversational tone.

"No, I'm not," I interrupted him. "It was just an excuse, a way to get close to you."

He clenched both fists. "You're in the wrong place to start cracking wise."

"I wouldn't dream of it. I just want to offer you a deal of a different kind."

"I'm listening."

"Fatjon Bytyçi. My friends and I had nothing to do with his death."

He changed expression. I had caught him by surprise. Until that moment, he was convinced that it was pure chance and my stupidity that had led me trustingly into his clutches. His plan was to pretend to sell me drugs and, when the time came for delivery, kidnap me, steal my money, torture me so that I'd tell him where Max and Beniamino were hiding, and then kill me.

"Why are you coming to tell me about it?"

"Because we know you've been looking for us. And not because you wanted to buy us a drink."

There was no mistaking the effect this had on him. I knew a lot, too much. He tried to find out more. "I still don't see where there's a deal in all this."

"Oh, there's a deal all right. It's an opportunity that'll change your life. What we can give you is the head—on a platter—of the guy who ordered the killing done. Take that back home and you can be a hero for your boss and for the whole family. This could be your chance to take Florian Tuda's place. And then if you tell your people we had nothing to do with it, we'll make you rich."

He shrugged, pretending a complete lack of interest. He needed time to recover from his surprise and to think it over carefully. "I don't understand if you're still interested in that certain merchandise."

"Nope."

"Then we have nothing more to talk about."

I stood up. "Think it over, Arben. Opportunities like this one come along once in a lifetime," I said, leaving a tiny scrap of paper behind me on the tabletop. On it I had written a phone number.

He didn't move a muscle. He just stood there and stared at me as if I were a piece of furniture. I put on my jacket and then my overcoat and walked out of the bar. I counted my paces as I walked and when I got to fifty I stopped, lit a cigarette, and discreetly took a glance behind me. As I'd imagined, Arben had sent one of his Maghrebi enforcers after me.

I crossed the piazza and turned toward Ponte Molino, before cutting into a bewildering medieval network of narrow streets. The guy had to pick up his speed to avoid losing me and, anxiously working to keep me in sight, he failed to notice Rossini, who was waiting for him, leaning casually against one of the columns supporting a portico. He smacked him hard in the face with the butt of his pistol. Twice. The man went down and lay there on the ground, motionless. I was no longer being followed.

"How'd it go?" asked Beniamino once he'd caught up with me.

"I think Arben swallowed the bait."

"And his greed will screw him."

"Let's hope so."

We met up with Max la Memoria who was waiting for us at a street corner in another part of town. He was loaded down with shopping bags.

"I feel like making something to eat," he explained.

We returned to our luxury apartment. The fat man busied himself in the kitchen, Beniamino hurried to his bedroom for yet another of his long and heartbreaking phone calls with Sylvie, and I sat down in front of the television set and started fooling around with the remote control. On one channel that was mostly about music, there was a tedious report on the recent transgressions of Amy Winehouse. I would have preferred to listen to her sing. That girl has a voice I like. Her treatment of *Back to Black* is just incredible.

I felt like listening to some good blues. I called Edoardo "Catfish" Fassio. He always knows everything that's happening in the world of the devil's own music.

"This evening, Claudio Bertolin is playing in an enoteca in Castelfranco Veneto; from what I've heard, he may even record the concert."

"Then I can't miss it."

"If you did, it would just be another of your many fuck-ups."

Max was larding a pork roast of remarkable size. "After a long period of abstinence, I'm going out to hear some good music."

The fat man looked up from the raw meat. "You talk to Beniamino about it?"

"Was there something scheduled?"

"I know that he wanted to go take a look at Stojkovic's office and house."

"No need for three of us. I did my part today when I talked to that human cesspool Arben."

"Right you are."

I watched him work for a while. Since the day we first met again in Lugano, we'd never talked about the past.

"I still haven't worked up the courage to go see what's taken the place of La Cuccia."

"Right now, the place is empty. For a while it was the usual sandwich shop, then a sushi bar, but nothing worked out."

My face lit up. "It's for sale?"

"I saw an ad in the newspaper a couple of days ago."

"It'd be nice to buy it again and start over. Once we're done with this fucked up story, I mean."

Max grimaced. "I don't know if I'm up for that, Marco."

"What do you mean?"

"I think I'll stay in Fratta Polesine. It's a good place for me. A lot of great people live there, there's still a sense of community that you can't find anywhere these days. For the first time, I feel like I'm surrounded by normal human beings, by friendship and kindness . . . And it's turning into a base for a lot of good projects."

"Are you thinking of getting back into politics?"

He smiled. "I'd like to give it a try, for the thousandth time in my life. They're trying to plunder Northeast Italy once and for all: they've got a succession of useless infrastructure projects and major public works that will finish off this part of the world for good. I don't feel like standing by and doing nothing."

"I have to admit I didn't expect this."

He sighed. "You thought it could all go back to the way it was?"

"No, the thought never passed through my mind. It's just that I'm not ready for the end of our partnership; I'm not ready for our lives to split up, whatever else happens."

"We were forced to pick up and leave one day. We lost everything we thought we owned. That's just what happened."

"I'm feeling a little lost, Max."

The fat man pulled open the fridge and uncorked a bottle of prosecco. "Bubbly, boy. You urgently need a pick-me-up."

"Is there a woman waiting for you in Fratta Polesine?"

"Her name's Irma. She showed up one day with some of my friends and she hasn't left since."

"Do you miss her?"

"I do. A lot."

I'd never seen the fat man making personal phone calls. "Why don't you ever call her?"

"I told her I'd come back."

"Sometimes that's not enough."

"I'm sick of mixing this shitty story with things that are good, you know what I mean?"

Max was in love. The bandit was in love. What about the Alligator? What about me? "Yeah, I think I understand," I replied after a little while. "Though I never made those kinds of distinctions."

"Yeah, but you have a few screws loose."

"Right, like you don't . . ."

He pointed at the floor. "I'm the only sane man in this place."

I gulped down three glassfuls in quick succession. Then I stood up and hugged Max. "I guess it just means I'll have to come visit you."

"As long as you don't ruin my reputation."

I stood up and put on my jacket. "Can I borrow your car?"

Max tossed me the car keys. "It doesn't belong to me; treat it nice."

I walked past Rossini's room. The door was half open, and I could see him staring out the window, his hands flat against the glass. I decided this wasn't the right time to bother him; I slipped quietly out of the apartment, gently pulling the front door shut as I stepped out onto the landing.

As soon as I got into the car, a little Korean compact that I was certain belonged to the mysterious Irma, I instinctively pulled open the glove compartment to see if I could find anything that would tell me about her. Then I slammed it brusquely shut. Poking into Max's love life was really going a bit too far.

I drove over to La Cuccia. I smoked a few cigarettes in the car, parked in front of a green for-sale sign with the name and logo of a real estate agency. It was depressing: shuttered, lightless, abandoned. I called Virna and told her where I was.

"Are you already nursing a bottle of Calvados?"

"No, these days I only drink at night, that is, if three glasses of prosecco in a row don't count."

"Why did you call me, Marco?"

"Because I suddenly realized that I'm all alone. And when all this mess is over and I can start living my life again, I'll have to deal with my solitude and loneliness."

"I hope you haven't taken me for just a shoulder you can shed your crocodile tears on."

"I'd never dream of it," I lied.

"Because I've had it up to here with men who trample everything and everyone in their path like rogue elephants until they hit fifty, and then start tugging at your sleeve and saying they feel sad."

"Virna, please, don't think that's what I'm up to; I haven't fallen that low."

"Good, that's a relief. So, I'm still waiting for you to answer my question: why'd you call?"

"To tell you that I'd like to start looking around for a nice place to live where a very attractive young mama could come spend a few enjoyable hours from time to time with yours truly."

"And that nice young mama would be me?"

"Right."

"Then you have to do things the right way and ask for my hand."

"Is that customary among lovers?"

"Especially among lovers. And you have to swear you'll be faithful to me."

"But you're not faithful to your husband."

"I need two men; you don't need two women. Or am I not enough for you? If not, we can just end this conversation right now."

"Virna, can I ask a question? Are you serious?"

"I certainly am. I have no intention of sharing you with another woman, and I don't want to discover that I have to spend time with a big cry-baby, which—let's face it—is exactly what many men your age are."

"Agreed. I'll do my best."

"No, you have to be certain. Give a call when you've made up your mind."

She hung up. What a force of nature.

I couldn't help it. I was still in love with her, and . . . I liked her. Just thinking about her stirred my baser instincts. I wanted a woman, and if I could, I'd have called Morena. She at least would have pretended to listen to me.

Instead, an hour later, her handsome policeman called me.

"Any news?"

"Nope."

"Then can you tell me what the fuck you were doing in the bar that the Peć Kosovars use as a front? I'm not sure I see how that fits in with our agreement."

I should have guessed that the place was under surveillance.

"You'll find out soon."

"Don't try to reassure me with bullshit, Buratti, because if there's anybody who'd be eager to replace the Serbs around here, it's those fucking Kosovars."

"My plans include a good fucking-over for Arben Alshabani, too, but first I have to make sure that no one's tailing me."

He mulled it over. The stakes were getting more interesting. "Fine. We've got a security camera trained on the bar, that's all."

"I'm not worried. But you have to relax too."

He emitted a dubious sigh. "Do I need to remind you what happens if you try to screw me?"

Jesus, what a pain in the ass! This whole thing was based on a card-castle of deceit and threats. "Now you're starting to annoy me."

"Whoa, take it easy, friend. You're the one who came looking for me."

"Just back off: I don't need you breathing down my neck."

"I'm afraid you're going to have to get used to the idea: I can do whatever I want because I'm the good guy."

I hung up the phone. Fucking cop.

The one phone call I was anxiously awaiting didn't come, though. Maybe we'd misjudged Arben. Maybe in the face of such a tough decision, he'd just decided to turn the problem over to the family.

What a shitty day. Nothing was going right. Max and Virna's words whirled through my mind. Between my legs was a pulsing need for pleasure and tenderness.

Nothing could save me now but the blues. It was still too early to drive to Castelfranco. I went to an out-of-the-way bar on the outskirts of town. It used to be a place where people went to find a little company without spending much money. The place looked the same, but now there were three young Chinese bartenders, two young men and a girl, ordered around sharply by a stern Chinese mother. And the clientele was different, too.

All things considered, that was okay with me. If the old crowd had been there, I'd certainly have wound up entangled in some tawdry one-nighter, and it would have just made me feel worse. I remembered I hadn't eaten yet; I ordered a panino and a beer. Then a pot of tea. The little café table sat next to the plate-glass window, right across from the bus stop, and I passed a few hours peering out at the serious, preoccupied faces of the passengers. I also saw two women I could have easily fallen in love with.

"Everything okay?" the owner asked me in broken Italian when I went up to the cash register to pay.

"Yes, just fine, but I could never become a regular customer of your bar. You see, watching one busload of people after another go by is deeply disturbing, and not the sort of thing I need at this particular point in my life."

The whole time I was talking, she never stopped smiling and nodding with patient resignation. All she wanted from me was a yes or a no. She hadn't understood a single word I'd said.

During the time I was in Switzerland, they had been busy building: new roads, roundabouts, and on-ramps. It was all just to get the semitrailers loaded with merchandise in and out more efficiently. Now, with the recession, traffic had declined. Still, I saved only about ten minutes. People were coming home from work, and there were cars everywhere you looked.

The first piece that Claudio Bertolin sang was *The Blues Is a Lonely Road*. I was unable to listen to the entire rendition of the second piece, *Have Been Down to Hell*, because my cellphone started buzzing annoyingly in my jacket pocket.

It was Arben. I reluctantly left the club. The bastard might as well have done it on purpose.

"We can discuss it," he said.

"Okay. Let's meet tomorrow morning at eleven in the shopping center on Viale Venezia. There's a bar on the ground floor."

"I would have expected something a little quieter, a little more out of the way."

Right, where you can kill some one in peace and quiet, with out-of-the-way comfort, I thought. "No offense, but I like my bars crowded and centrally located."

"Fine, but you have to give me a chance to check everything out, make sure you're clean."

"No problem."

I called Max. They were parked out front of the Serbian gangster's villa, and they were bored to tears. I gave him the good news.

"Then enjoy the rest of your evening. From tomorrow on we're on lockdown."

Two guitars, a bass, drums, harmonica, and vocals. Nine songs, plus the old standard *Every Day I Have the Blues*. It was a great concert. I went over and congratulated Bertolin, who had played a number of times at La Cuccia. I found him chatting with another Venetian bluesman, Marco Ballestracci. Marco gave me a copy of his latest CD, *Wimmen 'n' Devils*.

They asked why I'd closed my club. I fed them a plausible lie, and went over to the bar and ordered a Calvados. To my delight, I found they served Alligators.

I decided I'd have a single drink and I ordered a slice of cake.

"What kind?" asked a waitress in her early twenties, pointing to an overbrimming pastry trolley.

"You decide. I don't eat a lot of sweets, but I need to soak up a fair amount of alcohol."

"Then you'll need a double helping of chestnut cream tart," she decreed with the confidence of an expert. "Pastry dough soaks up alcohol like a sponge."

At last, I was happy. The blues were flowing through my veins like a healthful transfusion. The day had finally taken a turn for the better toward the end. But there was no one I knew there, and I missed the conversations at La Cuccia. I left before another wave of gloom could wash over me. When I got in the car, I slipped in the CD I'd just been given and pumped up the volume. *Baby Please Set a Date*, an old piece by Elmore James, exploded from the speakers.

I hadn't picked the bar in the shopping center at random. A former political prisoner I'd met in jail worked there. When he finally got out of prison, after about fifteen years inside, the woman he'd slept with the night before his arrest was out front, waiting for him. Other bandits, other loves. He couldn't do much with his engineering degree after all that time. So, now that the one purpose of his life was to take care of his wife and his baby daughter, born exactly nine months after his release from prison, he took a job as a waiter.

When we asked him to do us that favor, he agreed. No hesitation, no questions. He wasn't a guy with a faulty memory.

I arrived by cab and walked into the bar through a side entrance. Arben was already there, waiting for me. Arms crossed, watchful gaze. He gestured for me to follow him into the public restroom. We checked the stalls to make sure they were empty, and we searched one another for listening devices. We went back out into the bar, and I invited him to choose a table to sit at. Just one more piece of evidence of my good faith. Max had already sat down while we were in the bathroom, and with a pair of earphones and the daily sports pages, he looked like just another slacker with nothing to do. I tried to figure out who was there to protect the Mafioso, but none of the faces looked especially suspicious. If in fact he planned to accept our offer, he couldn't run the risk of showing up with bodyguards.

The waiter came over immediately and, of course, gave no sign of having ever met me. The Kosovar ordered a beer.

I asked for a cappuccino and a croissant. Arben wanted to begin negotiations immediately, but I told him it was better to wait for our orders to arrive, so that we wouldn't be interrupted. The real reason, though, was that the miniature microphone and recording device that would spell his downfall was hidden in the cardboard napkin dispenser, and I needed it to be brought to the table, on a tray, along with our orders, and placed in the middle of the table before anyone said a word.

The ex-convict played a perfect attentive waiter, and Arben, relaxed at last, swallowed a gulp of beer before asking me to explain the details of the deal.

"As I told you, we have nothing to do with the murder of Fatjon Bytyçi. To prove that, we can hand over to you the mastermind and we can give you the names of two of the actual killers. If you agree to persuade your people not to take revenge on us, we'll give you ten kilos of gold jewelry."

"You know too much about Fatjon's murder. It's hard to believe you had nothing to do with it."

I finished chewing my mouthful of croissant. Unhurriedly, savoring it. I wanted him to believe that I wasn't afraid of him. I wanted him to think I was stupid, not that I was tough.

"We've had two years to investigate, and we found out who did it. What we couldn't figure out was who fingered us for it."

He shrugged. "It was Agim, the younger brother. He came back to Peć with Fatjon's body, and told everyone that his older brother had been killed in a car crash. But inside the family, they knew that Fatjon had been killed over a woman. He'd stolen her from an Italian, and the Italian tracked him down, with the help of two friends, and he finally managed to find him somewhere in France. He made him pay for it in blood."

I sat up and listened carefully. This version had some interesting modifications. "How was he killed?"

"You really don't know?"

"I don't have the slightest idea."

"He was in a car, going home after a night out. They ambushed him in the open countryside. They killed Fatjon as well as his bodyguards."

"I don't understand why this Agim wouldn't have told the truth."

"Fatjon was a widower, but he was about to remarry. He was going to marry the daughter of the capo of another family."

So the true story of the gang bang parlor of Corenc had been concealed from everyone, even the members of the mafia family. Fatjon's father, the boss, and Agim wanted to make sure that nobody knew that the man who had been next in line to inferit the mafia empire of Peć, and who was about to establish an alliance with another mafia clan by marriage, was a depraved son of a bitch.

"So now Agim is going to marry the girl, right?"

"That's right. And together, the two clans will be much more powerful, but that's none of your business. Here's what I want to know: if I do agree to cooperate, how would the deal work?"

"It'd be very simple. We arrange a meeting, we hand over to you the mastermind, the names of the killers, and the gold. Just half the gold, of course. You'll get the rest when you prove to us that we no longer have a problem."

"So you and your friends are going to bring me the mastermind, giftwrapped with a bow on?"

"That's right, as a goodwill gesture. You can do what you want with him. Ship him home to Agim Bytyçi as a wedding present, or shoot him in the head."

He snickered. "You guys sure want to save your own skins."

"We know that you have a code of honor, and no one escapes it."

Pride broadened his smile. "Yeah, but I want all the gold. Otherwise you guys'll try to cheat me, say that we never had a deal."

Good old Arben, I thought. He'd already decided to kill us, so he knew he'd never see the second half of the gold unless he persuaded us to hand it all over immediately.

"Out of the question."

He stared at me, uncertain whether to try to argue or just settle for what he'd been offered.

I shook my head. "Don't push me on this. For that matter, I'm coming back to Padua to live, so there's no reason for me to try to trick you."

He had to let it go. Maybe he was mulling over the idea of postponing our executions so that he could lay his hands on all the loot.

"And I guess you wouldn't consider telling me the name of the mastermind."

"If I tell you, you'll just go get him on your own."

"This time I name the place."

"Fair enough. But it has to be in this part of town."

"No problem." He drained off the last of his beer and added: "Next time you beat up one of my men, make sure he's not a Kosovar."

"I don't know what you mean."

"Your friend broke a piece-of-shit Moroccan's jaw. That's not serious, but if you ever do anything of the sort to one of our people, get ready for a world of pain."

"That's pretty rough talk for two guys about to do business together."

"It's better to be clear from the beginning."

"That's fine. Let's just be clear that anyone who tails us does so at the risk of personal injury."

He gave me a hard glare. I could see in his eyes just how much pleasure he would take in murdering me. "Okay. Each of us has said what we needed to."

I let him leave first. A couple of minute later I stood up and left the bar, heading in the opposite direction. Max followed in my footsteps. As he strolled past the little table where I'd been sitting, he snagged the napkin-holder and came after me.

"The recording is clear as a bell," he said later, as we drove off together.

"It'll be a pleasure to screw that guy," I snapped. "He was sitting there talking to me, and the whole time he was thinking about how he could kill me. It was like being locked in a glass case with a rattlesnake."

"Now let's get ready for our second move."

"How many moves do you expect in this match?"

"Three. If it all works according to plan."

We drove to Treviso where we hooked up with Old Rossini, who had been staked out, maintaining an uninterrupted surveillance of Pavle Stojkovic since the night before. His eyes were red-rimmed and a scratchy white stubble covered his face. The car reeked of cigarettes and exhaustion. Max got in and sat in the passenger seat, next to Beniamino; I got in back.

"We can forget about trying to bust in on him in his nice country villa. The two enforcers live with him, he has guard dogs and a security system," he explained, pointing to an unsightly suburban apartment building. "You see the two plate-glass windows on the ground floor? That's the office of Balkan Market, and it's connected to the cellar warehouse by an internal staircase."

"His bodyguards?"

"They're with him every minute of the day."

"Anyone else?"

"A secretary. I thought I saw her go in this morning. When I called to check, a woman's voice answered."

"There must be someone in the warehouse."

"No. This morning I saw a couple of delivery vans arrive and leave, and Bozidar opened and closed the gates."

"What kind of car?"

"A black Mercedes, as usual It's parked in an underground garage. No way of getting to it."

"It doesn't look good to me," I said. "Maybe we should call Luc and Christine or the two Germans."

"No!" Beniamino hissed.

"If you want to get in there without getting badly hurt, you're going to need people who know how to handle a weapon. You can't do it by yourself."

"Oh, yes I can."

I leaned forward and said to Old Rossini: "You wouldn't by any chance be thinking of a convenient shootout where, after the smoke clears, all the bad guys are left lying on the ground, their chests riddled with bullets?"

He smacked the steering wheel angrily, his bracelets jangling. "Sometimes you can be a real asshole."

"Maybe so, but you know how these things can be. You knock on the door with the best intentions, but the other guy refuses to cooperate, he thinks he can get away with it, he tries to pull a slick move, and in the end, you have no choice but to start shooting."

He lit another in a seemingly endless series of cigarettes. "That won't happen."

I tapped the fat man on the shoulder. "What do you think?"

"Beniamino knows what he's doing. And the less we know about it, the better."

The Serbian gangster's bodyguards were veterans of a long and bloody civil war. They were also young and fast. But I would never have dreamed of bringing up any of those points. Rossini was still a legend, even at age sixty. Or sixty-two . . . He'd always been kind of vague about exactly how old he was, like an aging actress.

"I bow to the wishes of the majority," I said, playfully, to cut the tension. "Now what do we do?"

"We sit here, bored out of our skulls, waiting to figure out when the time is ripe to go pay a visit on our old friend Pavle."

"You don't think that three men sitting in a parked car might be a little obvious?"

Rossini rapped his knuckles on the window. "Smoked glass. You can't see a fucking thing from outside."

After a while it started raining.

"There's been more rain this year than I can remember," I muttered.

Rossini and the fat man exchanged a glance and burst out laughing.

"What? What did I say?"

"You really went senile living in Lugano. Now you're starting to comment on the weather, like an old guy on a park bench. This is Beniamino, and I'm Max. We're not old guys sitting on a park bench next to you."

They had a point. They were my only real friends. But I was still uncomfortable about what the fat man had said to me the day before. I felt weird, as if I'd lost my way in a network of streets that I knew like the back of my hand.

"Yesterday I spent three hours sitting in a bar run by a Chinese family watching people get on and off of buses."

"Now that's the Marco I know," the old smuggler broke in, as he continued to snicker. "You're the only guy I know who could waste so much time on such futile bullshit."

"Futile? Now I can offer you the benefit of my pearls of wisdom about life."

"I'd bet money we're going to hear all about it."

"You'd be grateful to me as long as you live."

At 12:45 on the dot, the three Serbians and the secretary came out of the building. Pavle Stojkovic walked ahead, accompanied by a woman aged somewhere between 35 and 40. She was tall, she had long black hair, and she was dressed in a somewhat ostentatious style. Bozidar and Vladan followed a few yards behind them. They walked about 150 feet and stepped into a bar that served quick lunches.

"Secretary and lover," Rossini decided.

"Did they arrive together?" I asked.

"No. The woman arrived shortly after him."

"We should do what we can to keep her out of this."

"That may not be possible."

"One more fucking problem," I muttered. I was sick of sitting in a parked car with the windows rolled up.

Max craned his neck to look back at me. "Don't nag, Marco. You know we wouldn't hurt a hair on her head."

Forty-five minutes later, they went back into the offices of the Balkan Market. Same formation.

Between 2 and 5 o'clock, two more delivery vans pulled up, completely unmarked. Each stayed less than twenty minutes.

Half an hour later, the Mercedes revved up the ramp from the cellar parking area and pulled up to the front door. By the light of a streetlamp, we saw that only the bodyguards were in the car. Pavle and his secretary came out an hour later. She took care of locking the door and turning on the security system. Then the woman got into an expensive sports car. The Serb waved goodbye with a smile.

I looked at my watch. "Six thirty on the dot."

"These people are methodical," said Max. "Everything to the minute, every blessed day they do the same things at the same time. We could sit here for a year watching them: nothing would change."

"The delivery vans," Beniamino mumbled. "Three of them this morning, two more this afternoon. We'll use one of them to get in."

The next morning we followed the first van when it pulled out from the underground ramp at the Balkan Market. It pulled onto the highway and didn't get off until the first exit for Verona. It led us to an ordinary-looking industrial shed way out in the countryside.

"I have to say I'd love to know what kind of 'Balkan merchandise' Pavle Stojkovic's company sells."

Rossini shrugged. "I don't have the slightest idea. You can't even tell who delivers and who picks up the merchandise."

"If it's illegal, it means that our friend has more than one guardian angel. What cop wouldn't want to know a little more about an import-export firm called Balkan Market?"

"Maybe the police have a surveillance camera on the place, like they do on Arben Alshabani's bar."

Rossini snapped his fingers. "I hadn't thought of that. Maybe we should be a little more careful."

We were basically going to just lower our heads and charge in: we didn't have a real plan, we didn't even have a vague idea of what we might be running into.

We went back to Treviso after lunch. Max insisted on getting off the highway near Vicenza, where he knew a good little trattoria.

That afternoon no vans pulled up to the Balkan Market. Otherwise, everything went exactly like the day before.

"Let's try following them," I suggested when I saw Pavle getting into the Mercedes.

Rossini wasn't convinced. "If they spot us, it'll fuck everything up."

"Maybe they're going to do some grocery shopping."

"Oh, can you just see someone like Stojkovic pushing a shopping cart in a supermarket?"

"He has to eat."

"His housekeeper takes care of it," Beniamino snapped. "We need to focus on the delivery vans."

It took us four days to figure out that the van that showed up at the warehouse most frequently was a light-blue Renault.

The van would drive down the ramp and stop in front of the door, under the vigilant lens of a videocamera. After a couple of minutes, one of the goons would open the door and let the van drive in. The driver was a young man with long hair and a series of tiny earrings piercing his right ear. He lived with his wife and two children not far from Montebelluna and he drove all over the Veneto region making deliveries. He didn't look like a gangster; he probably had nothing to do with any criminal activity. All the same, we were going to have bust into his life rather roughly.

It happened the day that we decided to go ahead and settle some scores with that bastard Pavle Stojkovic.

E ven though it had turned spring two days ago, it was still bitterly cold. It was seven thirty in the morning, and there was nothing to suggest that winter was coming to an end. The guy back-and-forthed his delivery van to drive out of his front yard. He turned down a country lane and, a few hundred yards further along, came upon our car pulled carelessly to the side, so that it partly blocked the thoroughfare. Max, Beniamino, and I were leaning over, intently studying the left rear wheel.

The guy stopped the van about thirty feet short of the car, and leaned his head out the window. "Need help?"

Rossini walked toward the van and brought a handgun up, level with his chin. "This is going to be a special day for you."

The driver didn't look particularly frightened. "The van's empty and I have 150 euros in my wallet."

"Your name is Fabio, right?" the old smuggler asked him in a fatherly tone of voice.

"Yes . . ."

"Well, Fabio, we need your van. Later, we'll let you know where you can go pick it up."

"I need it for my job."

"We'll pay for your time."

"You're not going to kidnap me and keep me tied up somewhere, are you?"

Beniamino smiled reassuringly. "No, you're going to go back home and wait for our phone call, safe and sound with your wife and children."

The young man turned white. All we'd had to do was mention his family to strike terror into his heart. I wasn't proud of it, but we couldn't afford to have him report the van as stolen. That's exactly the kind of crime that gets the cops interested.

Max recited his phone number by heart. "That's right, isn't it?"

Fabio gulped. "I'll do whatever you want, but . . ."

"You just behave yourself, and nothing will go wrong," I reassured him. Then I pointed toward his house. "Go back to bed, pull the covers over your head, and stay warm. You have a headache and a fever today."

He walked off unsteadily, and then started running. We were behaving like a bunch of amateurs, but that might have been lost on Fabio. He might just have fallen for our bluff.

Beniamino climbed into the driver's seat, and then stepped out of the van waving a clipboard with a beer-bottle-shaped clip; on it was the list of the day's stops.

"Balkan Market, 9:30 a.m."

The fat man got in the car with Old Rossini. I got in the Renault delivery van and followed them. At a stoplight, I glanced at myself in the rearview mirror. I was dressed in a jacket and tie and was cleanshaven. This was starting to become a habit. I looked like the owner of a small manufacturing company substituting for an employee who was out sick. No one would have noticed anything odd. That was just Northeast Italy.

When we got to Treviso my friends parked the car and climbed into the back of the van, where they hid with the tool bag. When it was time for Fabio's stop I drove up the ramp that led to the warehouse. I lowered the sun visor and pretended to blow my nose, but Bozidar was satisfied once he recognized the van.

He began walking the heavy gate open on its rollers without noticing that Beniamino had already gotten out and was coming behind him with a pistol in one hand. He jammed the barrel of the gun hard against the small of the Serbian bodyguard's back and Bozidar stiffened, raising both hands. There was enough room for me to get by, so I revved the motor and drove the van past the gate. Once we were inside the warehouse, Max got out too. We were in a cellar, roughly a thousand square feet, the walls lined with metal shelves filled with large cardboard boxes.

After Rossini ordered the bodyguard to kneel down, the fat man and I tied him hand and foot with plastic pipe-fasteners. It was an Israeli method. No way he could get free. We gagged and blindfolded him, then we dragged him into a corner.

He put up no resistance. He was a professional and he knew when it was time to admit the enemy had him outnumbered. In the meantime, Beniamino had been keeping an eye on the internal staircase. We climbed up, step by step, soundlessly, and we emerged into a small windowless room, perfectly bare except for a desk and chair; on the desk sat the monitors of four surveillance cameras. One of the monitors showed Bozidar rocking back and forth, trying to get off his back and onto one side. Two others were monitoring the exterior, and the last one showed a hallway. We exchanged alarmed glances. Had Vladan seen what was happening and sounded the alarm?

Rossini shook his head. It was too quiet; no one knew we were there. He kept moving forward, pistols leveled. We followed a few steps behind him. We could clearly hear the voice of the woman talking on the phone. Before long, we could glimpse her through a door that had been left ajar. We could tell Vladan was there because of his habit of whistling as he made tea. He must have been inside the little corner kitchen, and there was no way to sneak up behind him.

Beniamino materialized at the kitchen door, two .45s aimed at his midsection. "You don't want to die this morning, do you?" he said softly.

The battle-hardened veteran rapidly calculated his chances of surviving the situation he was in; he ran and reran the odds in his mind, but he couldn't see a way of avoiding one or more bullets. He spread both arms to signal his surrender, but Rossini hadn't forgotten from their last encounter that Vladan had a dagger concealed up his sleeve. "Pull it out with two fingers."

The bodyguard froze in surprise and looked at him quizzically.

"Bozidar told me," Rossini lied, treacherously.

Vladan would never forgive his fellow bodyguard. Actually, we'd noticed when Vladan made a move for the dagger up his sleeve during our meeting in the pastry shop in Vicenza. These are things that you can't forget, even years later.

The Serbian obeyed and extracted a commando stiletto, flat, short, and lethal. He laid it on the table. Rossini ordered him to turn around and get down on his knees. Max and I giftwrapped him like his partner.

"You two go take care of the woman. Bring her to Pavle's office."

The secretary, still absorbed in her phone conversation, hadn't noticed a thing. She spoke good Italian but she was obviously Serbian. As soon as she hung up the phone, we walked into the room, with our hands in our pockets.

The woman's reaction dispelled any doubts we might have had that she was a member of the gang: she didn't scream, she certainly didn't look like she was about to faint.

She was pretty, but her facial features were a little harsh, and tension didn't help. "Who are you two?"

"Come with us. Let's go have a chat with your boss."

She didn't make us say it twice. She walked ahead of us down the hall, then she opened a door. The office was expensively appointed. The Serbian gangster was seated at his desk, both arms extended, both hands flat on the mahogany writing surface. Rossini was sitting across from him, both Colts resting on his thighs. He pointed the woman to a sofa.

"Sit down over there."

"So all of you decided to show up," Pavle hissed contemptuously. "Not even a shred of brains."

Beniamino gave him a withering glance. "Our good friend was just asking me why we were paying him this ill-mannered surprise visit."

"What did you tell him?" asked the fat man.

"That he's making a mistake by continuing to consider us a bunch of idiots."

Now it was my turn. "Do you want to continue down this road? Are you looking to die, or would you rather negotiate?"

"I imagine that I'm going to die no matter what I do."

"You'd deserve it," snarled the old smuggler.

I unbuttoned my overcoat. It was hot, and I would gladly have taken off my latex gloves, too. "Sure, we'd be delighted to murder you, but we made a deal with the Kosovars of Fatjon Bytyçi's family. So we're going to hand you over to Agim, Fatjon's little brother."

The woman started talking rapidly in Serbian, with a thin piercing voice. Only a wave of Beniamino's pistols managed to shut her up. I hadn't taken my eyes off Pavle. I wanted to enjoy the instant of pure terror that would wash over him when we informed him he'd be handed over to the Kosovar Mafiosi. Instead, I thought I detected a flicker of relief in his eyes.

It didn't add up.

I grabbed the woman by the arm and turned to Max.

"Let's find a place to lock her up."

We found a tiny windowless closet filled with office supplies. "If Pavle won't talk, we'll come back to see you," I threatened her.

We wouldn't do it in any case, so she was bound to believe that her boss and lover had betrayed her. She just gave me a scornful glance. We turned the key in the lock and, to make doubly sure, tipped a chair back under the door handle.

"You've got to imagine these people have been through the mill. They are tough-skinned, no question about it," Max commented.

"There's something wrong here. Let's try to figure this out."

"What do you mean?"

"Why isn't Pavle terrified at the idea of winding up in the hands of the Kosovars?"

"I just told you: they've got balls and a willingness to be martyrs."

"How did they manage to get word to Agim Bytyçi that we killed Fatjon?"

"I don't know. Maybe just putting out word was sufficient."

I wanted to smoke, but I resisted the impulse. There are plenty of people in prison because they left traces of DNA on cigarette filters dropped in the wrong places. "I don't know how to explain it, but I'm pretty sure that the Serb's not afraid of Agim Bytyçi."

"I have a hard time believing it, but if you're right, what do we do?"

"Let me improvise."

We went back into the office. Stojkovic was exactly where we'd left him; he hadn't moved an inch. I watched him closely for a few more seconds and then decided to go ahead and listen to my instincts; I'd rely on the impressions of the moment.

"We want to know where Greta Gardner is."

He cleared his throat. "Like I told you before, we weren't able to find out anything about her."

"Have you ever heard the name of Arben Alshabani?"

He shook his head. "He must be a Kosovar."

"That's right. And he's a profoundly stupid young man who runs the Peć family in this region, because his boss, Florian Tuda, wound up in prison. He can't wait to get his hands on you; he's hoping to give his old boss and Agim a nice surprise by sending them your head and your hands in a box. Get it? He's the only one who knows that we're here right now."

He clenched his fist once, and then twice. Maybe his confidence was beginning to waver or perhaps, much more simply, his arms had gone numb. I decided to take a chance.

"If we leave here without you, he'll come in with his knife and cut you all to pieces. What do you think he'll do to the woman? And do you think that when you beg him to talk to Agim he'll listen to you?"

I could feel my two friends staring at me. They must be thinking I'd lost my mind.

But my instincts had been right. The question Stojkovic asked proved it.

"What are you offering me?"

"Escape," I lied. "Only you get out of here. Your bodyguards and the woman belong to Alshabani."

"Her name is Slavka and I'm not giving her up. I'm not leaving here without her."

The love of a Serbian gangster. He was ready to die for his sweetheart, but he'd taken no pity on Sylvie. This was neither the time nor the place, but I couldn't help but asking him: "Why don't you two live together?"

"She's married to an Italian."

I looked at Beniamino, who shrugged. "All that matters to me is to get him to talk."

Then I turned to Max, who nodded in agreement. "Arben'll have to settle for the two enforcers."

"What do you want to know?" Pavle asked.

"The truth," I answered. Then I realized the stupidity of what I'd just said. Someone like Stojkovic didn't even know the meaning of the word: Truth. If he did, he'd never tell it. He would cautiously restrict himself to what he judged strictly necessary to ensure his own safety and freedom. I'd better try to be a little more precise.

"We want to understand how we got dragged into this mess, and we also want information that'll help us track down and neutralize Greta Gardner."

Unobtrusively, Max pulled a small tape recorder out of his pocket and turned it on.

The former intelligence service officer sat silently for a few seconds. Once he'd collected his thoughts he started telling a story. From the beginning. From long-ago 2004.

The Serbian intelligence service wanted to uncover the truth about the theft from the Institute of Legal Medicine in order to make the Kosovars an international laughingstock, and they sent two active agents into Italy.

The guy who wanted to coerce us into working for him, and who had done everything he could think of to get Rossini to murder him, was named Milan Markovic. He was Greta Gardner's boyfriend, from her university days, when she was studying and he was keeping an eye on the students to make sure they didn't get any inconvenient ideas. The strange cross-shape that we'd noticed on his ring was a reproduction of the cut that they'd carved in their flesh with a kitchen knife so that they could mingle their blood, right after making love for the first time.

Milan, ten years older than her, was handsome but certainly no genius. We had proof of that from the way he'd provoked us into murdering him.

The brains of the couple was Greta. Her real name was Natalija Dinic, but only Pavle knew that, because he had enlisted her in the intelligence services on Milan's recommendation. After personally overseeing her training, he had sent both of them out of Serbia. Then the civil war had come, and the pair of agents had carried on operations under the banner of Greater Serbia.

After Pavle left the intelligence service to become a gangster, he lost sight of them. He had heard that after Milan was killed and the operation failed, Greta was expelled from the intelligence service. She changed careers, devoting herself to the profitable business of high-end prostitution. In short order, she had created a small but very efficient organization capable of catering to any fantasy that happened to flit through the mind of a wealthy man. And when he said "any fantasy," Stojkovic specified, he meant even the most taboo and diseased fantasies.

In the meantime, she had continued to nurse her thirst for revenge. She was waiting for the right opportunity to present itself. That's exactly what happened when Pavle began dealing with Agim Bytyçi on a regular basis. Top secret dealings, given the wall of hatred that separated the Serbs and Kosovars.

Agim had no intention of murdering his brother, at least not at first. At least not until the prospect of his brother's wedding appeared on the horizon. The girl who had been promised as Fatjon's bride was madly in love with Agim; he was just as much in love with her. Agim could never have tolerated the idea of his beloved in the hands of that depraved beast.

"I'll take care of it," Pavle Stojkovic had told him, and he'd begun to organize the plot, putting to use the experience he'd developed in many years of honorable career in the intelligence services of, first, Yugoslavia, and later, Serbia.

He'd reached out to Greta. She'd immediately come up with the idea of offering Fatjon the unprecedented thrill of running a gang bang parlor. In fact, the Kosovar gangster was notorious not only for his fondness for mature and sensual women, but also for group rapes, and so . . .

I turned sharply to look at Rossini, certain that he was about to pull the trigger.

Beniamino's hands were wrapped around the grips of both his pistols, but his index fingers were far from the triggers. Two fat tears dropped from his eyes, running down his cheeks.

"That's the story," Pavle concluded. "Do you want the details?"

"Spare us the details," Beniamino answered, his voice cavernous with grief and pain.

Greta's love. Agim's love. Pavle's business affairs. What a fucked-up mess.

By the way: "What kind of business dealings do you have with the Kosovar?" I hastened to ask.

"Well, I guess I can tell you now. I'm pretty sure I'm going to have to change careers."

The Serbian gangster led us down into the warehouse. Without so much as a glance at his bodyguard, bound, gagged, and blindfolded on the floor, he picked up a box cutter and opened a large cardboard box, tipping its contents out onto the floor: packaged pharmaceuticals.

Max picked up one of the brightly printed packages. "This is an antiviral medicine for bird flu."

"It's all counterfeit merchandise," Stojkovic explained, waving at the shelves. "The first ones we developed were counterfeit Viagra and other pharmaceuticals to cure impotence, then we went on to anti-diabetic drugs and medicines for cardiac diseases . . . Most of it we sell on the internet, but the operation is growing, and now we can sell these things anywhere. They're really popular among illegal immigrants, because they're afraid to go into legitimate clinics and hospitals. They're made in Kosovo. Agim has started up a number of labs, with Indian and Pakistani chemists. He's a smart young man. He got a degree in economics at an American university, and he came back home with modern ideas . . ."

I heard the sound of a pistol being cocked. Rossini had thumbed back the hammer and was aiming one of his .45's right in the Serbian's face. "I just got over my misgivings about breaking our agreement."

I stepped into the line of fire. "He still has to tell us how to track down Greta Gardner."

"Counterfeit pharmaceuticals: I'm sorry, that's just too shitty to let him live."

"I agree with you, but we have to choose what we care about most, what's most important for Sylvie."

"Right, Sylvie. I'd like to remind you that this is the son of a bitch who dropped photographs of my woman in the mailbox, and then pretended to understand the pain I was feeling." With a sharp gesture, he lowered his pistol. "If I ever meet you again, Pavle, I promise I'll kill you."

The Serbian drew a deep sigh of relief. It hadn't been a very smart idea to brag about the fake medicine ring.

Max went to get the woman and brought her down into the cellar store room. He pulled a duffel bag out of the back of the van and opened it. "Now the two of you, take what's in this duffel bag and put it into these two sacks."

The woman plunged her hands into the duffel bag and pulled out bracelets, necklaces, and rings. "It's gold."

The Serbian did the same thing and understood. "With our fingerprints on it."

I complimented him. "You're a smart boy."

"Where's it from?"

"According to eyewitnesses, the armed robbers spoke in Serbian. I think it'd be a good idea to get as far from here as possible."

I looked at my watch. "It's time to go. Arben Alshabani will be here soon. You just have enough time to tell us exactly how to find Greta Gardner."

He reeled off an address in Paris and a cover name.

"You aren't shitting me, are you?"

"You're going to have to take my word."

I gave him a nasty grin. "And so will you, because now you're going to join your lovely Slavka in the supply closet. The story about the Kosovar arriving was just a fairytale to get you to sing."

He showed no sign of surprise. He did nothing more than to mutter that this wasn't part of our agreement.

"In a couple of hours, you ought to be able to kick down the door and get out of here."

Beniamino jabbed him in the back with his pistols. "Get going, piece of shit."

Max pushed the play button on the tape recorder. The sound of Pavle's voice confessing his arrangements with Agim Bytyçi cut through the air.

Stojkovic spun around, his mouth twisted into a bitter grimace. "I should have known."

"You forget we ever met, or this recording goes on YouTube."

"Don't worry. I've been playing this kind of game a lot longer than you."

The fat man and I hid one of the sacks behind the cardboard boxes; it contained five kilos of finished gold jewelry. Then we climbed aboard the delivery van and got the hell out of that cursed place.

I lit a cigarette and called Attilio Carini, the handsome policeman. "Okay, I'm going to give you an address in Treviso. Get there fast, and you'll find a nice little pigsty. I recommend that you be the first one in the door, if you want to make it look more believable. But I guarantee you'll come out smelling like a rose . . ."

"Fine. Give me the damn address."

"One last thing: I'm going to need you to make sure that the surveillance camera out front of the bar where Arben Alshabani hangs out is out of order for the next twenty-four hours."

Beniamino stopped the van outside of a toy store; a little while later he came out with two enormous stuffed animals. He'd taken it to a ridiculous extreme, like all the bandits of his generation.

"These are for the children of Fabio, the guy that loaned us the delivery van."

All the evening news shows led with reports of a major operation by the police forces of Padua and Treviso who had arrested a gang of Serbians who were trafficking in counterfeit medicines and fencing stolen gold jewelry. The police raids had resulted in the recovery of two kilos of assorted jewelry from the multimillion-euro robbery committed some time before in a goldsmith's workshop in Valenza, in the province of Alessandria.

"The cops went shopping," I snickered. "Almost four kilos of jewelry for wives, girlfriends, mothers-in-law."

"But what about poor little Pavle?" Max asked sarcastically while he was piling our plates high with *gnocchi al ragù* he'd made with his own pretty hands. "When the Maronite Lebanese come around to ask him about their gold, hard time in prison is going to get a little bit harder for him . . ."

"That asshole is the kind of guy who comes out on top no matter what," Beniamino pronounced his opinion. Then he turned to me. "Now, how are you going to screw the Kosovar?"

I poured myself a glass of wine. A red tocai from the Colli Berici. "Not sure. Do you have any ideas?"

The next morning, the Kosovar was playing cards with a few of his minions. "I want to have a word with you."

He made a gesture and everyone else scattered.

"I brought you the gold," I said, extending a small bag to him under the table.

"Who the fuck told you to bring it here?" Arben blurted out in annoyance.

He was rapidly trying to think what to do next. His people would ask him what I'd brought to him in the bar, the least secure place in all Padua. And he wasn't an idiot. The reports of the police sweep in Treviso were front-page news in all the local papers.

"Yesterday they find gold in the hands of those shits the Serbs and this morning you bring a bag of it here to me. Did you bring the cops with you too?"

"No. But the terms of our deal have changed. We thought that Pavle Stojkovic was the mastermind behind Fatjon's murder; well, we were wrong, and we don't accuse people of murders they had nothing to do with. And anyway, the police beat us to him."

The Kosovar looked at me in puzzlement. What I was telling him wasn't even slightly believable, but right then and there it didn't much matter.

"We're giving you the gold, and it's only half of what we promised; in exchange we need you to go to Agim and tell him that you're sure that we had nothing to do with his brother's death. And you're going to have to be convincing, very convincing, because your job is to get your boss to retract the death sentence that's out on us."

I pulled a mini CD out of my overcoat pocket and laid it down next to his glass of beer.

"What's that?"

"A copy of the audio recording of our chat in the bar in the shopping center the other morning."

He turned pale. Then a surge of fury made his eyes glaze over as he scrabbled with one hand, grabbing for the jacket pocket that held his switchblade knife.

"Don't try it," I hissed, doing all I could to conceal the fear that was clawing at my stomach. "My friends are waiting outside, and they came heavy. You'd never leave here alive."

He shrieked a sequence of insults in his native tongue; everyone in the bar turned to stare at us.

"Calm down and try to think. We're not trying to screw you; we just want to be left in peace."

"Get out; never let me see you around here again."

I stood up. "One last piece of advice: melt that jewelry down in a hurry. It's way too easy to identify; and you don't want to get dragged into the trial alongside the Serbs."

Then I walked hastily out the door. Rossini emerged from behind a pillar in the portico where he'd been hiding. He'd been lurking there with Max; thanks to the miniature microphone glued to my chest, they'd listened to the whole conver-

sation with Arben. If he'd decided to disembowel me, Beniamino would have been inside the bar to stop him in plenty of
time. At least, that was the plan . . .

I lit a cigarette; my hands were trembling. I was really getting sick of all this.

The old smuggler smiled. "And we're through with another
one."

Once we were back in the car I turned my cell phone back
on. There were a dozen messages from Attilio Carini. I called
him back.

"Pigsty doesn't begin to cover it. I had to work miracles to
stay out of trouble myself," he complained.

"Don't bust my balls. I saw you on TV. I read about you in
the newspapers. You're the most famous cop in all of Northeast
Italy."

"You promised you'd give me Alshabani, too."

"Yeah, well, that one didn't work out so well."

"You can keep working on it till it does . . ."

"No. It's time to say goodbye."

"I decide when that time has come."

Cops. I closed my eyes and counted to three. Cops are
always the same. "You want to play kid games? You want to see
who can piss farther, whose dick is longer? Come off it!"

He started laughing and hung up. I took the SIM card out
of my cell phone and tossed it out the window. At the next stoplight, I gave the phone to a flower peddler.

"If you want to know the truth," Rossini snapped, "I don't
like trading favors with the cops. I'd like to avoid that if we
can."

"No, you should really say a prayer to the god of crooked
cops," I shot back argumentatively. "It's not the way it used to
be, when you always knew who you were dealing with and you
could just run things without dealing with the police. Your
problem these days is getting information, and the cops are the

best source available. They gather information, collect it in a central location, and it's always for sale."

"Plus," added the fat man, "all these organized crime families and rings of Mafiosi just use the cops to eliminate their competitors. It's just one big stew, a pot of marmalade. You can't make distinctions the way you used to be able to."

The old smuggler took one hand off the wheel to jangle his bracelets. "That's exactly the thing. If you want to avoid drowning in this sea of shit, you have to live in the past. Find others who think the way you do and work as an archaeologist of the underworld: smuggling and old-school knockovers. The problem has always been your fucking investigations, Marco. There you are, just stirring shit from dawn to dark. When this mess is over, I really hope you decide to change your line of work."

He was taking it out on me and me alone, even though Max had been my partner in investigations. Evidently the fat man had talked to him about Fratta Polesine and Irma. This wasn't the time to talk about such things. Especially because it was the last thing I felt like doing.

"And exactly how does this mess end? We still haven't talked about how to deal with Greta Gardner."

"As far as I'm concerned, I'm going to go to Paris, scope out the situation, kill her, and go home to Sylvie."

"What about you?" I asked Max.

"Maybe we've saved our own asses and settled some scores," he said, looking out the window. "If my presence isn't truly indispensable, I'd just as soon stay here."

Old Rossini gripped his arm affectionately. "This is the last act. We'll do fine just the two of us."

I pretended to object. "Whoa, whoa, why do you assume I'm coming with you?"

"Because you don't have a fucking thing to do here."

Natalija Dinic, alias Greta Gardner, alias Ivana Biserka, was a beautiful woman. In the xerox of her passport she looked like a pale little blonde. In the flesh, she was a woman that my friend the sax player Maurizio Camardi, an unrivaled connoisseur of beautiful women, would have described admiringly as a "cherry bomb." She was spectacular, provocative, deeply appealing. According to my calculations, she had to be exactly forty. She looked it and in some sense she flaunted her age. But one thing was certain: even men much younger than her would have thrown themselves at her feet.

When we saw her for the first time, we were astounded. Beniamino sat open-mouthed, incapable of making the slightest sound. She looked disturbingly like Sylvie. And there was no mistaking the fact that this had been a conscious choice, pursued single-mindedly, with the assistance of more than one plastic surgeon.

I gathered my courage and finally asked Beniamino: "What really happened?"

He grimaced, shutting his eyes as if a bolt of pain had stabbed through his body. "Before they handed her over to Fatjon Bytyçi, my love was the 'guest' of that bitch for a period of preparation. She used violence on Sylvie, she humiliated her and forced her to dance, to wear ridiculous costumes."

"Sylvie told you this?"

Rossini shook his head. "She won't talk to me about any of what happened."

"So how did you find out?"

"The notebook. It's got graph paper, like the notebooks little children use. There's a pair of squirrels on the cover. Cute as can be. But read it and it takes you straight to hell. I think it was her shrink's idea."

After a few days of cautious tailing, we had established that wherever Greta went, she was accompanied by two women. One of them drove the long black limousine with tinted windows, the other was always next to her, as if she were a bodyguard; sometimes she acted more like a secretary, at other times it seemed as if she were an intimate friend.

The driver was the younger of the two women. She had close-cropped blonde hair, she was petite, and she drove as if she'd had a steering wheel in front of her since she was a baby. Maybe she really had. The other, older woman was a typical Slavic beauty, perhaps a Russian: high cheekbones, long hair, a physique that had been sculpted in a gym, or very likely in the exercise yard of a military barracks. She had a way of moving that is typical of people who use violence professionally. Unlike Greta, who was wore dizzyingly high heels, both women wore rubber-soled flats.

One evening I browbeat Beniamino into phoning Sylvie in my presence. "Ask her!"

"It's pointless cruelty."

"We have to know."

A few minutes later, he was gripping the cell phone, white knuckled. "Was Greta Gardner alone, or were the two women with her?"

Sylvie had burst into a torrent of sobs. Rossini held the phone up to my ear so I could hear her. It was heartbreaking.

"Happy?"

I spent a sleepless night, but I had to know if those two women were her accomplices. The situation demanded it. For the next two days, the old smuggler pretty much refused to speak to me. I took advantage of that to go out at night. I took a walk through the quarter we were in, and found myself outside a theater. Big posters announced a concert: Mauro Palmas would offer a musical portrait of the colors of the mistral wind. Allowing myself to be lulled by the king of winds would only do my heart good; I bought a ticket. It was money well spent. For two hours, the sound of the cantabile lute and the mandola helped me to forget I was in Paris on serious business.

All three women lived together in a luxurious apartment not far from the cathedral of the Madeleine; but the church that Greta attended regularly was Serbian Orthodox, and was dedicated to St. Sava of Serbia. It was in the 18th arrondissement, at number 23, Rue du Simplon. That day in May she was going to be married in that church. Or, perhaps we should say, she had hoped to be married to a certain Vule Lez, age 48, a native of Belgrade. It was enough to type his name into a search engine and it became clear that he was a notorious nationalist gangster.

We were unable to find out anything more than that. We learned very little about her life or her business. She moved around the city and traveled frequently; at times she'd vanish for two or three days at a time. Tailing her was complicated and very dangerous. Paris is patrolled by serious-minded and very aggressive policemen. Hanging around a street door or busy corner for too long meant the police were sure to notice you. When you're getting ready to kill somebody, it's the dumbest mistake you can make.

Beniamino and I were living in a little rat's nest not far from the Gare de Lyon. The long days we'd spent tailing a woman who looked like a clone of Sylvie had been psychologically grueling.

The decision to kill her the day of her wedding had been Beniamino's. I was against it. I preferred the idea of shooting her as she left her house; I didn't really care if we had to murder the two other women. They wouldn't be much of a loss for mankind. But Rossini wanted to administer poetic justice, he wanted an exemplary punishment. He would sneak out from behind the priest in the middle of the wedding ceremony and shoot down Vule and then Greta, in cold blood, at the altar.

That was the plan. We'd developed it as we studied the church down to the finest details. Often there were concerts; choirs singing Byzantine, Serbian, and Russian liturgical chants; we took seats in the last rows of pews, listening distractedly, observing very attentively.

The morning of Friday, May 15 we'd stolen a car on the far side of Paris. It was a light-fingered theft, done on the fly with perfect technique. A woman had parked her small car next to a newsstand, engine running, keys in the ignition. She'd just stepped away for the thirty seconds it took to buy a newspaper. Just as she was paying the newsvendor, she noticed out of the corner of her eye that two figures had climbed into her car. Too late.

We drove to the church and we checked out our escape route. The next day, Beniamino would call me and speak a few words into the phone: "I'm going in now."

I'd drive out of the parking lot in the Rue du Mont Cenis and turn right down Rue du Simplon. Then I'd pick up Beniamino as he left the church in the aftermath of the double murder, and turn left onto Rue des Poissonniers; another left in Rue des Amiraux, and finally a right turn onto the Boulevard Ornano, which I'd take all the way up to the Metro station of Porte de Clignancourt. There we'd disappear into the endless underground of Paris.

And in fact that part of the plan worked beautifully. Rossini fucked up everything else.

I waited for him outside the church. I had arrived half a minute early, and I heard a single distinct pistol shot. Beniamino came running out of the church, both pistols leveled. Except for his sunglasses, he was dressed in white from head to foot. He got into the back seat and I took off, tires screeching.

"What the fuck happened?"

"I killed him," he replied as he began changing his clothes. "They had just been pronounced man and wife."

"What about Greta?"

"She got down on her knees and covered her face with her veil."

"What did you do then?"

"I just couldn't bring myself to pull the trigger."

"But why, Beniamino? Why the fuck did you let that whore trick you again?"

My eyes blurred from the anger and disappointment; I came within inches of broadsiding a taxi. "You know what happens now? They're going to start looking for us again. We're back where we fucking started, back where we were at the beginning of 2006."

"I thought I was looking at Sylvie, kneeling there in the church," he confessed in a whisper.

We abandoned the car, discarded our clothes and pistols in a trashcan, and descended into the tunnels of the Paris Metro system.

The evening news shows and morning papers gave considerable play to the reports of the murder at the altar. But neither the widowed newlywed nor the very few wedding guests spoke to the press, and the media circus soon broke down the big top and moved on, dismissing the killing as a feud between Serbian factions: the dead man's criminal record helped to make that version of the facts more believable.

I phoned Max. "Despite everything, the sun is still shining."

"Here too. It's nice and warm."

"Where are you?"

"At the Chiosco, with Pape, Giorgio, and Walter from Cagliari."

"So you've had a spectacular meal."

"Oh, yes. Marzia was cooking."

"I hear a tremendous racket. How many of you are there?"

"About fifty. It's the annual banquet of the Union of Rationalists, Atheists, and Agnostics."

I didn't think I'd ever heard of the organization in question, but I didn't want to start asking questions. I said nothing.

The fat man cleared his throat. "I don't know whether to be pissed off or concerned. In any case, I'm not happy."

"For what it's worth, there are extenuating circumstances."

He sighed loudly. "I think there's more to it than that. He's made her a widow twice now, and her anger and grief will make her very, very dangerous. We know perfectly well what she's capable of doing . . ."

"So?"

"So the old man couldn't help but know that when he had her in front of him in the church."

Instead of leaving Paris, we continued to follow Greta. We watched the funeral from a safe distance, too, and I couldn't help but admire the sober elegance of her small black hat. It was exactly the same style as the one worn by Ceca, Arkan's widow, the day of his funeral.

A few days later we saw her go into a restaurant on Rue de la Reine. She was no longer dressed in mourning. The driver remained in the car, the other woman sat at her side. The restaurant was small and their table was next to the front window. Sitting with them was a man with the distinctive appearance and demeanor of a professional soldier.

I felt a rush of shivers running down my back. "She's hiring him to wipe us out."

Beniamino shrugged. "I'd bet he's the guy who kidnapped Sylvie."

The tone of voice with which he said those words triggered my first suspicions. "By the way: what did Sylvie say about the fact that you spared the life of the woman who had her kid-napped and held her captive in a gang bang parlor?"

"Well, she didn't insult me the way you did . . . She said that every cloud has a silver lining, and that we could take advantage of the situation to dismantle the network of this organization and rescue the women who are trapped in its coils."

I slapped my thigh. "I should have figured it out before now."

"Figured out what?"

"That Sylvie asked you not to murder her."

"Well, you could say that was her general stance."

"And you couldn't bring yourself to say no, even though you knew it was fucking insane; you just hope that if you go along with what she asks, she might recover and become the woman she once was."

"You think I did the wrong thing?"

Bandit love.

"No. I'd have done it too, but that woman is cruel, ruthless, and diabolical. She'll hunt us down and chop us into pieces."

He sank his nails into my shoulder. "No. We're going to be hunting her, and we won't let up for a second until we've shattered her little empire."

So that was his plan. "You could have at least asked me if I wanted to sign up for your war."

"Why? Would you have refused?"

"It's crazy, Beniamino."

"This is a tumor that has to be eliminated."

I sighed. "And who says we're the surgeons for the job?"

"I say so. And this time, we're not going to bring cops and Mafiosi into it. We'll do this our way."

"We're old school gangsters, relics of a past that's gone for-ever. They'll eat us alive."

"Then go back to Lugano and sit on your park bench while I clean up this mess."

"No, fuck, there's no way I can leave you to do this on your own; who knows what kind of a mess you'd get into this time."

Out of the corner of my eye I could see Old Rossini with a cunning smile on his face. Son of a bitch. Max had seen it all.

The guy stood up and took his leave of Greta Gardner with a hasty but formal kiss on the hand. He left the restaurant and walked away. We gave him a fifty-yard start and started tailing him.

He was a professional and it wouldn't be long before he noticed us and recognized us. He'd think we were amateurs who didn't even realize we were doing his job for him. Maybe he'd smile to himself, or tell himself that this was his lucky day.

It would never cross his mind that the old smuggler and armed robber walking by my side just wanted him to know that he wasn't hiding anymore, and that in order to keep a promise made to his love, he'd be risking his life according to rules that none of his enemies knew or could understand. This was bandit love. I'd follow him to the end because I lacked any love so compelling or powerful; I had nothing that tied me to a single person or place. And after all, Rossini is my friend. One of the only two friends I still have. And in a world where everyone's busy fucking everybody else that has to count for something.

THE END

ACKNOWLEDGMENTS

The author would like to thank Edoardo "Catfish" Fassio, Ernesto Milanesi, Luca Barbieri, Elena Battista, and Heman Zed.

Massimo Carlotto is the author of *The Fugitive*, *Death's Dark Abyss*, *The Goodbye Kiss*, and most recently, with Marco Videtta, *Poisonville*, all published by Europa Editions. His novels have enjoyed great success outside of Italy, and several have been made into highly acclaimed films.

Carmine Abate
Between Two Seas
"A moving portrayal of generational continuity."
—*Kirkus*
224 pp • $14.95 • 978-1-933372-40-2

Salwa Al Neimi
The Proof of the Honey
"Al Neimi announces the end of a taboo in the Arab world: that of *sex!*"
—*Reuters*
144 pp • $15.00 • 978-1-933372-68-6

Alberto Angela
A Day in the Life of Ancient Rome
"Fascinating and accessible."
—*Il Giornale*
392 pp • $16.00 • 978-1-933372-71-6

Muriel Barbery
The Elegance of the Hedgehog
"Gently satirical, exceptionally winning and inevitably bittersweet."
—Michael Dirda, *The Washington Post*
336 pp • $15.00 • 978-1-933372-60-0

Gourmet Rhapsody
"In the pages of this book, Barbery shows off her finest gift: lightness."
—*La Repubblica*
176 pp • $15.00 • 978-1-933372-95-2

Stefano Benni
Margherita Dolce Vita
"A modern fable...hilarious social commentary."—*People*
240 pp • $14.95 • 978-1-933372-20-4

Timeskipper
"Benni again unveils his Italian brand of magical realism."
—*Library Journal*
400 pp • $16.95 • 978-1-933372-44-0

Romano Bilenchi
The Chill
120 pp • $15.00 • 978-1-933372-90-7

Massimo Carlotto
The Goodbye Kiss
"A masterpiece of Italian noir."
—*Globe and Mail*
160 pp • $14.95 • 978-1-933372-05-1

Death's Dark Abyss
"A remarkable study of corruption and redemption."
—*Kirkus* (starred review)
160 pp • $14.95 • 978-1-933372-18-1

The Fugitive
"[Carlotto is] the reigning king of Mediterranean noir."
—*The Boston Phoenix*
176 pp • $14.95 • 978-1-933372-25-9

(with Marco Videtta)
Poisonville
"The business world as described by Carlotto and Videtta
in *Poisonville* is frightening as hell."
—*La Repubblica*
224 pp • $15.00 • 978-1-933372-91-4

Francisco Coloane
Tierra del Fuego
"Coloane is the Jack London of our times."—Alvaro Mutis
192 pp • $14.95 • 978-1-933372-63-1

Giancarlo De Cataldo
The Father and the Foreigner
"A slim but touching noir novel from one of Italy's best writers
in the genre."—*Quaderni Noir*
144 pp • $15.00 • 978-1-933372-72-3

Shashi Deshpande
The Dark Holds No Terrors
"[Deshpande is] an extremely talented storyteller."—*Hindustan Times*
272 pp • $15.00 • 978-1-933372-67-9

Helmut Dubiel
Deep In the Brain: Living with Parkinson's Disease
"A book that begs reflection."—*Die Zeit*
144 pp • $15.00 • 978-1-933372-70-9

Steve Erickson
Zeroville
"A funny, disturbing, daring and demanding novel—Erickson's best."
—*The New York Times Book Review*
352 pp • $14.95 • 978-1-933372-39-6

Elena Ferrante
The Days of Abandonment
"The raging, torrential voice of [this] author is something rare."
—*The New York Times*
192 pp • $14.95 • 978-1-933372-00-6

Troubling Love
"Ferrante's polished language belies the rawness of her imagery."
—*The New Yorker*
144 pp • $14.95 • 978-1-933372-16-7

The Lost Daughter
"So refined, almost translucent."—*The Boston Globe*
144 pp • $14.95 • 978-1-933372-42-6

Jane Gardam
Old Filth
"Old Filth belongs in the Dickensian pantheon of memorable characters."
—*The New York Times Book Review*
304 pp • $14.95 • 978-1-933372-13-6

The Queen of the Tambourine
"A truly superb and moving novel."—*The Boston Globe*
272 pp • $14.95 • 978-1-933372-36-5

The People on Privilege Hill
"Engrossing stories of hilarity and heartbreak."—*Seattle Times*
208 pp • $15.95 • 978-1-933372-56-3

The Man in the Wooden Hat
"Here is a writer who delivers the world we live in…with memorable and moving skill."—*The Boston Globe*
240 pp • $15.00 • 978-1-933372-89-1

Alicia Giménez-Bartlett
Dog Day
"Delicado and Garzón prove to be one of the more engaging sleuth teams to debut in a long time."—*The Washington Post*
320 pp • $14.95 • 978-1-933372-14-3

Prime Time Suspect
"A gripping police procedural."—*The Washington Post*
320 pp • $14.95 • 978-1-933372-31-0

Death Rites
"Petra is developing into a good cop, and her earnest efforts to assert her authority…are worth cheering."—*The New York Times*
304 pp • $16.95 • 978-1-933372-54-9

Katharina Hacker
The Have-Nots
"Hacker's prose soars."—*Publishers Weekly*
352 pp • $14.95 • 978-1-933372-41-9

Patrick Hamilton
Hangover Square
"Patrick Hamilton's novels are dark tunnels of misery, loneliness, deceit, and sexual obsession."—*New York Review of Books*
336 pp • $14.95 • 978-1-933372-06-

James Hamilton-Paterson
Cooking with Fernet Branca
"Irresistible!"—*The Washington Post*
288 pp • $14.95 • 978-1-933372-01-3

Amazing Disgrace
"It's loads of fun, light and dazzling as a peacock feather."
—*New York Magazine*
352 pp • $14.95 • 978-1-933372-19-8

Rancid Pansies
"Campy comic saga about hack writer and self-styled 'culinary genius' Gerald Samper."—*Seattle Times*
288 pp • $15.95 • 978-1-933372-62-4

Seven-Tenths: The Sea and Its Thresholds
"The kind of book that, were he alive now, Shelley might have written."
—*Charles Spawson*
416 pp • $16.00 • 978-1-933372-69-3

Alfred Hayes
The Girl on the Via Flaminia
"Immensely readable."—*The New York Times*
164 pp • $14.95 • 978-1-933372-24-2

Jean-Claude Izzo
Total Chaos
"Izzo's Marseilles is ravishing."—*Globe and Mail*
256 pp • $14.95 • 978-1-933372-04-4

Chourmo
"A bitter, sad and tender salute to a place equally impossible to love
or leave."—*Kirkus* (starred review)
256 pp • $14.95 • 978-1-933372-17-4

Solea
"[Izzo is] a talented writer who draws from the deep, dark well of noir."
—*The Washington Post*
208 pp • $14.95 • 978-1-933372-30-3

The Lost Sailors
"Izzo digs deep into what makes men weep."—*Time Out New York*
272 pp • $14.95 • 978-1-933372-35-8

A Sun for the Dying
"Beautiful, like a black sun, tragic and desperate."—*Le Point*
224 pp • $15.00 • 978-1-933372-59-4

Gail Jones
Sorry
"Jones's gift for conjuring place and mood rarely falters."
—*Times Literary Supplement*
240 pp • $15.95 • 978-1-933372-55-6

Matthew F. Jones
Boot Tracks
"A gritty action tale."—*The Philadelphia Inquirer*
208 pp • $14.95 • 978-1-933372-11-2

Ioanna Karystiani
The Jasmine Isle
"A modern Greek tragedy about love foredoomed and family life."
—*Kirkus*
288 pp • $14.95 • 978-1-933372-10-5

Swell
"Karystiani movingly pays homage to the sea and those who live from it."
—*La Repubblica*
256 pp • $15.00 • 978-1-933372-98-3

Gene Kerrigan
The Midnight Choir
"The lethal precision of his closing punches leave quite a lasting mark."
—*Entertainment Weekly*
368 pp • $14.95 • 978-1-933372-26-6

Little Criminals
"A great story…relentless and brilliant."—*Roddy Doyle*
352 pp • $16.95 • 978-1-933372-43-3

Peter Kocan
Fresh Fields
"A stark, harrowing, yet deeply courageous work of immense power and magnitude."—*Quadrant*
304 pp • $14.95 • 978-1-933372-29-7

The Treatment and the Cure
"Kocan tells this story with grace and humor."—*Publishers Weekly*
256 pp • $15.95 • 978-1-933372-45-7

Helmut Krausser
Eros
"Helmut Krausser has succeeded in writing a great German epochal novel."—*Focus*
352 pp • $16.95 • 978-1-933372-58-7

Amara Lakhous
Clash of Civilizations Over an Elevator in Piazza Vittorio
"Do we have an Italian Camus on our hands? Just possibly."
—*The Philadelphia Inquirer*
144 pp • $14.95 • 978-1-933372-61-7

Lia Levi
The Jewish Husband
"An exemplary tale of small lives engulfed in the vortex of history."
—*Il Messaggero*
224 pp • $15.00 • 978-1-933372-93-8

Carlo Lucarelli
Carte Blanche
"Lucarelli proves that the dark and sinister are better evoked when one opts for unadulterated grit and grime."—*The San Diego Union-Tribune*
128 pp • $14.95 • 978-1-933372-15-0

The Damned Season
"De Luca…is a man both pursuing and pursued. And that makes him one of the more interesting figures in crime fiction."
—*The Philadelphia Inquirer*
128 pp • $14.95 • 978-1-933372-27-3

Via delle Oche
"Delivers a resolution true to the series' moral relativism."—*Publishers Weekly*
160 pp • $14.95 • 978-1-933372-53-2

Edna Mazya
Love Burns
"Combines the suspense of a murder mystery with
the absurdity of a Woody Allen movie."—*Kirkus*
224 pp • $14.95 • 978-1-933372-08-2

Sélim Nassib
I Loved You for Your Voice
"Nassib spins a rhapsodic narrative out of the indissoluble
connection between two creative souls."—*Kirkus*
272 pp • $14.95 • 978-1-933372-07-5

The Palestinian Lover
"A delicate, passionate novel in which history and life
are inextricably entwined."
—*RAI Books*
192 pp • $14.95 • 978-1-933372-23-5

Amélie Nothomb
Tokyo Fiancée
"Intimate and honest...depicts perfectly a nontraditional romance."
—*Publishers Weekly*
160 pp • $15.00 • 978-1-933372-64-8

Valeria Parrella
For Grace Received
"A voice that is new, original, and decidedly unique."—*Rolling Stone* (Italy)
144 pp • $15.00 • 978-1-933372-94-5

Alessandro Piperno
The Worst Intentions
"A coruscating mixture of satire, family epic, Proustian meditation, and erotomaniacal farce."—*The New Yorker*
320 pp • $14.95 • 978-1-933372-33-4

Boualem Sansal
The German Mujahid
"Terror, doubt, revolt, guilt, and despair—a surprising range of emotions is admirably and convincingly depicted in this incredible novel."
—*L'Express* (France)
240 pp • $15.00 • 978-1-933372-92-1

Eric-Emmanuel Schmitt
The Most Beautiful Book in the World
"Eight novellas, parables on the idea of a future, filled with redeeming optimism."—*Lire Magazine*
192 pp • $15.00 • 978-1-933372-74-7

Domenico Starnone
First Execution
"Starnone's books are small theatres of action, both physical and psychological."—*L'Espresso* (Italy)
176 pp • $15.00 • 978-1-933372-66-2

Joel Stone
The Jerusalem File
"Joel Stone is a major new talent."—*Cleveland Plain Dealer*
160 pp • $15.00 • 978-1-933372-65-5